Running Away

Running Away

a novel by

Harriett Gilbert

HARPER & ROW, PUBLISHERS
New York, Hagerstown, San Francisco, London

J
G

RUNNING AWAY

Library of Congress Cataloging in Publication Data
Gilbert, Harriett, 1948–
    Running away.

    SUMMARY: After a series of crises, a 16-year-old girl in an English private school learns to take control of her own life.
    [1. School stories]   I. Title.
PZ7.G3737Ru   [Fic.]   79-1937
ISBN 0-06-021972-6
ISBN 0-06-021973-4 lib. bdg.

For Nadia

Part I

I

It was an ordinary Tuesday. It began as did every Tuesday, as did every day in the school, with the clanging of a cracked handbell down the dormitory corridors, with the yawns, gasps and squeals of ninety awakening girls, with the under-matron's swelling call of "Wake up, wake up now, time to get up" and the slap of bare feet against thin bedside rugs.

Then came chapel, breakfast, assembly, the morning lessons and lunch. There was no break in the timetable, no swerve from its preordained progress; no hint, no whisper of danger on that ordinary Tuesday morning.

When lunch was finished, the dining-room tables cleared, grace spoken, Jane Rackham trooped with the rest of the school to the glass-domed entrance hall to await the duty-mistress and the post tray. They did this every day; except for Sunday, when there was no post. With Audrey Croft, Jane pushed as close as she could to the heavy, hexagonal table where the duty-mistress would stand to call the names.

"Why on earth do I bother?" she asked. "I never get *anything* this early in the week. My mama usually writes on Thursday, or Friday. I might just as well not bother to come."

"Why *do* you, then?" asked Audrey, raking the fringe from her forehead, trickling slivers of blue-black hair through her fingers.

"What else do you suggest? Rush off and get changed for games? The choice isn't exactly scintillating, is it?"

It was, if anything, a Tuesday more boring than usual.

The duty-mistress was Mrs. Bailey. Freckled, plump, short, shortsighted, she waddled into the glass-domed entrance hall.

"All right, girls, come on, we'll have a bit of hush, shall we?"

Silence, as intense as the March sunlight dropping through the glass-domed ceiling, as insistent as the lingering smells of cabbage and lamb stew, overcame the entrance hall.

Stillness also, as Mrs. Bailey stood the wooden post tray on the table and took from it the first letter.

"Beverly . . . Mathewson. Beverly Mathewson? Who's Beverly Mathewson?"

"Matterson!" the girls called, frustrated, impatient, but excited, knowing the game.

"There's no need to shout. Beverly *Matter*son!"

The pale-blue envelope sped from upstretched hand to upstretched hand, dipping and leaping towards its intended recipient.

"Ntosake Ebounike!"

4

"No problem reading *that* one, naturally," whispered Audrey.

Jane smiled.

Then it was that Mrs. Bailey called, "Jane Bacham? Beaching?"

And Jane jumped. And Jane shouted, "Rackham! It's me, Mrs. Bailey. Here!"

The flat, white package bounced towards her on its thrusting conveyor belt of hands. It was extraordinary. Who could it be from, on a Tuesday? Not her mother. A sister, then? An aunt?

Jane snatched the envelope and fumbled it face upwards; then stopped, confused. The address had been typewritten. No one whom she knew typed their letters to her. For a moment, she felt as though her own words, her own boredom had challenged this mystery into existence and was frightened.

Then she realized. She turned towards Audrey.

"I think it's from my father," she said.

Her father used a typewriter. He'd written to her only twice in the five years she'd been at boarding school, but the letter must be from him.

"I wonder what's happened to make *him* break his vow of silence?"

But Jane Rackham didn't believe that anything terrible had happened, not as she pushed her index finger along the tunnel between envelope and flap, not as Mrs. Bailey continued her shortsighted incantation and the Spanish maids laughed, rattling their trollies of dirty crockery from the dining room to the kitchen, not as she levered her finger to rip the envelope open.

5

Darling Janey,

You'd have thought, after all the practice she's had, that your mama would've been able to produce her seventh child without any problems at all, wouldn't you? Well, she must have got a bit overconfident this time because, instead of having the new baby at the end of April, as we were all expecting, she went and had it two days ago, about six weeks prematurely.

Now THERE IS NOTHING FOR YOU TO WORRY ABOUT. I mean that, darling. Both mother and child are fine, as they say in the newspapers. They're in hospital, of course, but will be coming out as soon as the baby's a bit bigger and stronger—it's being kept in a sort of human's aquarium at the moment, catching up on the growing it should've been doing inside your mama.

As for the rest of us, your awful brothers and sisters and me, we're surviving as best we can, though I'm not quite sure how long we'll last out, as the Home Help Agency has managed to send us their No. 1 Gestapo Lady—all bristling mustache and iron-clad bosom and knife blades in the toes of her boots. On top of which, she's an alcoholic. A bottle of Scotch (*my* Scotch) a night is as nothing to her. But we encourage this intemperance because, when she's not flat on her back hiccuping, she's out in the kitchen concocting terrible, poisoned suet puddings, which we *have* to eat because she watches over us from first spoonful to last, swishing a studded cat-o'-nine-tails against her calves as she does so.

So, you see that you're well out of all this and, by the time you get home for the holidays, Frau Himmler should have

gone, your mother + baby returned and everything be back
to good old normal. In the meantime, my love and kisses,

Your affectionate

Papa.

Jane looked up. Audrey had gone. Mrs. Bailey had long
disappeared around the bend in the wide, marble stairway
that led up to the staff room and, of the ninety girls, only
some prefects remained. These were clustered around a
postcard, giggling and punching each other between the
shoulder blades. Their backs were turned to her. She
walked away quietly, so that they should not swivel their
badge-proud chests in her direction and call out, "What are
you still doing here, Jane Rackham? Aren't you supposed
to be at games or a lesson or something?"

In the wall halfway down the wooden stairs that led to the
school basement and the changing rooms, there was a cubbyhole the size and shape of a large tea chest. Jane climbed
into this and rested her back against its wooden paneling.
From close behind her rose the sounds of girls changing for
games: yells of despair at the loss of a lacrosse boot, accusations of theft, accusations of uncleanliness.

"For goodness' sake, Bummly, those socks could stand
up by themselves. Come and feel Bummly's socks, everybody; they're solid."

Jane closed her eyes and blocked her ears, trying to create
privacy from her own resources, like an ostrich. But the
harder she pressed with her fingers, the tighter she clenched
her lids, the greater became the black, beating confusion so
violently released inside her head.

7

She opened her eyes. The normality of pastel-green paint, of brown industrial linoleum, of striplighting and of water pipes slung low along the belly of the ceiling reasserted itself. She drew the letter once more from its envelope.

"Darling Janey ... THERE IS NOTHING FOR YOU TO WORRY ABOUT. ... So, you see that you're well out of all this. ..."

With a spasm of pain, she screwed it into a ball. She crushed it between the fingers and palms of her hands, astonished, terrified by the force of her body's hatred.

Hatred? No, that was mad, that was ridiculous. Hate? Hate what? Hate whom?

She gasped. The inrush of air sent soaring, for a moment, the weight that was smothering her brain. With logic, with thought, with words, she hurried to fill its place.

She'd been surprised, that was all. Shocked. And it was normal that she should be shocked. Her mother had had her baby six weeks early and the two were still in hospital. *Any*one'd be upset by that.

But it was going to be all right. There was no need to worry. She'd been told, there was no need for her to worry.

And what did it matter that she should've been going home next Saturday, for a weekend out? What did it matter that now she couldn't, that now she'd have to stay behind in school? Nothing. It didn't matter at all. Nor did it matter that her father'd forgotten she was even supposed to *be* coming. He'd other concerns: her sisters, her brothers, the drunken home help. Jane *saw* all that.

So she was all right. Everybody else was all right. She'd been told not to worry. Well then, she wouldn't. She wouldn't.

Jane's eyes began to refocus on the pastel-green paint of the basement stairwell, on the wooden steps, on the banister rails. Her hands began to unclench.

When they were quite relaxed and open, she smoothed back to flatness the warm, crumpled paper of her father's letter. But she didn't reread it. Instead, she folded it into thirds and replaced it as fast as she could inside its envelope. Then she rolled her weight onto one hip and buried the envelope in the pocket of her skirt. Yes, everything was going to be all right. There was no further need for her to worry.

Meanwhile, meanwhile Tuesday was continuing around her. She must hurry to get changed for games. After games would come French Conversation, then tea, then prep, then supper. . . .

"Plain! For goodness' sake! What're you doing lounging around in there? You do know we're supposed to be on the games field five minutes ago, don't you?"

Audrey Croft's face stared up through the banister rails. The metal bars had squashed her pink cheeks towards each other and distorted her plump lips into a sneer. From her left hand, a lacrosse stick trailed on the floor.

"Don't tell me you've got your period," she said.

"Not very likely, is it?" said Jane. "Twice in two weeks? I'm not a hemophiliac."

She untucked her legs and swung them down onto the steps. Other girls had emerged from the changing rooms and, heavy with woolen sweaters and rubber-soled boots, were passing through the basement on their way to the side door that led to the drive and the games fields.

Audrey asked, "Well, are you going to tell me what

9

you're up to, or not? It doesn't bother me."

"I'm not up to anything," said Jane.

She began to unbutton her shirt sleeves.

She said, "My mother's just had her baby," not looking up as she said it, concentrating on the cuff of her shirt, on the button that was refusing to release itself.

"Liar! You said it wasn't due till the end of April."

"I know. She's had it prematurely. About six weeks prematurely."

"What do you mean?"

"Early, you ignorant cow. Premature means early."

"I know *that*. But *why* did she? What went wrong?"

"*Nothing* went wrong," said Jane. "There's no need to make a melodrama out of it. She just had it early, that's all. They're both fine."

"Let me see the letter," said Audrey.

Jane looked at her.

Audrey'd rested her lacrosse stick against the stairs. She was tucking back her hair and pulling the sleeves of her games sweater from her wrists.

Jane said, "I've told you what was in it."

"I know. I just want to see it."

"Why? It's nothing. It's . . ."

"Okay. So why can't I see it?"

"You *can* see it."

"Give it to me, then."

Snatching it out of her pocket, Jane handed the letter to Audrey.

"It got a bit crumpled," she said. "I dropped it. And for goodness' sake, don't take any notice of the jokes. That's just him being stupid."

10

"I expect he does it automatically," said Audrey.

Jane's father was the television critic for a national Sunday newspaper.

Then Audrey laughed.

She said, "I bet he's making all that up, about the Home Help woman. He's jolly funny."

Jane smiled with her mouth. She waited. The basement door banged against its jamb, then shuffled, once more, ajar. From the games fields floated the high, wavery sound of a whistle. From the kitchen, somewhere above her head, came a muffled hubbub of laughter and female, Spanish voices and knives clatter-clattering against knives.

She said, "Come on, it's not a book. It's only a one-page letter, for heaven's sake."

A feeling like impatience, like nervousness, was beginning to make her jiggle her foot and drum the banister rail with her knuckles.

She said, "You see, I told you. It's all okay. Oh, *now* what're you doing? You don't have to read it twice, for heaven's sake. Nobody's asking you to learn it by heart. Aug, give it to me. We're going to get into trouble. I'm not even *changed* yet."

"Don't snatch. And don't flap like that. You look like a pig when you get worked up. Hey, Plain, you're not *worried*, are you?"

"No!" said Jane.

She said, "The only nuisance is, I'm going to have to miss my weekend out. That's all. Look, go on. Hurry up. I'll see you up there in a minute."

Yanking her sweater up over her head, she went down the stairs into the changing room.

In front of her locker, she stopped. She pulled the door open. She rolled her sweater into a ball and thrust it to the back of the shelf. Then, after a second's pause, she threw the letter in with it.

Turning, she saw that Audrey had come up behind her.

"Now what's the matter?" she asked.

"Nothing. I'm just waiting for you."

"You don't *have* to."

"I know that. Look," said Audrey, "you could always come out with me, next weekend, I suppose."

"What?"

"You're not deaf, are you? Or do you want to stay here? I mean, there's that talk by a West African missionary on Sunday, with *slides.* Maybe you don't want to miss that?"

"Don't be stupid."

Jane sat on the floor to lace her lacrosse boots.

Audrey said, "Well? What do you want? A written invitation?"

"No, of course not," said Jane.

She tugged at the stringy, black laces and gritted her teeth.

Of course she didn't want a written invitation. Of course she wanted to go out for the weekend with Audrey. In the four years that they'd been best friends, neither one had asked the other to her home.

Jane remembered how elegant and beautiful had seemed Audrey's mother, when glimpsed at a Sports Day or a Prize Giving; how tall she'd seemed and well dressed, with her long, painted nails and her hair, dark like Audrey's, swept back from a high, bony forehead. It'd be marvelous to meet

12

Mrs. Croft, to talk with her, to stay in her London flat; marvelous, also, to meet Audrey's older sister, Henrietta, who'd been at the school years before, whose prize-winning paintings still hung in the art room and who now had a job, as a makeup artist, in television.

To meet these glamorous women who were Audrey's family, to see Audrey's home, her bedroom, her books and records and the stereo she'd been given last Christmas, all these were things for which Jane had never dared hope. Yet, now that they were being offered to her, now that Audrey was offering them to her like a casual gift, she hesitated, torn between accepting and refusing.

It was the invitation's connection with her father's letter that troubled her, the way in which it revived the unease that she'd thought she'd buried at the back of her locker shelf. It was so un*like* Audrey to think of asking her out; so un*usual.*

Jane looped the stringy, black laces and jerked them into a bow.

"Well?"

"What?" she said.

"*Well.* D'you want to come or don't you? Look, you're not just trying to make yourself interesting or something, are you? Because, you'd better believe me, I really couldn't care less *where* you spend your damn weekend."

"Okay," said Jane. "Then don't go on about it."

"Fine. And remind me never to offer you anything again."

"It's not *that.*"

"What? Not what? You don't even know what you're

talking about, do you? Well, I just hope you have a smashing time. Because, I can assure you, *I* will."

"It's too late, anyway," said Jane, unhooking her lacrosse stick, unhooking her yellow sports sweater, slamming the door to her locker and turning round.

"What is?"

"To arrange it with your mother and so on."

"We'll ring her now."

"How?"

"We'll go and ask the Termite if we can use the office telephone."

"She'll never let us."

"Of course she will. It's an emergency."

"It *isn't*," said Jane. "It isn't. Why on earth did you say that?"

"Because, thickhead, if we *don't* say that, we *won't* be allowed to use the phone. God, you're so stupid sometimes you make me want to hit you. Now, are you coming or aren't you? And don't just stand there mumbling and saying it doesn't matter when she asks you if it's really important, or I shall, I'll strangle you, I promise."

Audrey grabbed the neck of Jane's sweater and, suddenly, as though a weight had been shoved from her brain, as though a blackness had fallen away to reveal ordinary, bright, familiar colors, Jane dropped back her head and laughed.

"God, Aug," she said, "you're such a sweet-*natured* person. D'you know that? Such a pacifist! Such a lady! But, hey, hey, look, what're we going to do about these clothes? We can't go up there like this."

14

"Why not? We're supposed to be playing lacrosse, aren't we? It shows our good intentions. And I've just had a thought. If we take our time over this, we might miss games altogether."

2

The Termite was Miss D. M. Anthony, the headmistress. A dry, tight, monochrome woman, with graying hair scraped back from a hard, gray face, she conducted her affairs from an impersonal and humorless drawing room on the ground floor of the school.

The drawing room's furniture—its filing cabinets, its glass-fronted bookcases, its mahogany writing table and broken, sagging armchairs—seemed all to have died from boredom a long, long time ago. Only the Termite's cats, her beloved cats, were alive, as they sprawled and curled and lurked in the dismal room's every corner.

In one of the armchairs, a large, tabby tom lay flat on his back, attempting, by means of various neck contortions, to clean his stomach.

A tortoiseshell-and-white she-cat sat with her nose pressed against French windows, one ear twitching, both eyes concentrated on a sparrow that hopped its thoughtless way across the terrace outside.

Beneath the mahogany writing table, a young black-and-white male opened wide his sharp-toothed mouth, stretched, relaxed, closed his mouth, then wandered out into the open. Abruptly, he grabbed with both front paws the top of the table leg nearest to him and furrowed the polished wood with his claws.

A neat, colorless hand descended to tap his rump.

"Don't *do* that," said Miss Anthony. "You're a naughty boy, Aziz."

The headmistress leaned forwards and down from her chair, one hand extended, and said, "Here. Here, boy. Come here."

She rubbed her thumb against the tip of her first two fingers. She made a ticking noise with her tongue. The kitten approached to investigate.

"He's really pretty, isn't he?" said Audrey.

Miss Anthony smiled. She scrubbed the kitten's head with her knuckles. Then, replacing her hands in front of her on the writing table, she said, "Well, Jane. So how many of you does that make now?"

"Sorry, what?" asked Jane, who'd been engrossed in watching the kitten.

"How many *children*, now, in the family?"

"Oh! Er, six," said Jane. "Well, no, seven; with me."

"Seven? And all girls? Surely not. What about the next one down?"

"The next one down from me? Yes. Yes, she's a girl."

"But not yet old enough to join us here, I gather."

"Well, she is, you see, only she doesn't like boarding school. I mean, she's never *been* to boarding school, but . . . I'm the only one who goes to boarding school. Well, so far, anyway . . ."

"I see. And what about the latest? The impatient one?"

"What?" asked Jane.

16

"Don't keep *saying* that. Please. And please take your hands from your pockets. That's better. Now, what was I saying? Yes, the new baby. Is it a boy or a girl?"

"I don't know," said Jane, shrugging, looking down at the carpet.

She heard the headmistress sigh.

She heard Audrey say, "Plain only heard about it this afternoon, Miss Anthony. That's why we were wondering whether you couldn't *possibly* let us use the office telephone. . . ."

In the middle of the carpet, the black-and-white kitten flipped suddenly onto his back and clapped his front paws together, trying to catch a fly. Jane removed her attention to this, to the grace of the animal's movements, to the uninhibited, guiltless way that he attempted murder on the Termite's drawing-room floor. Let Audrey do the talking, the charming. Jane would've liked to kneel beside the kitten, to stroke his soft, arched stomach, to rub the hollow behind his ear and make him purr.

"Thanks a *lot*, Miss Anthony. That's really super. And we'll be as quick as we can, honestly."

"That's all right, Audrey. It's most kind of you to have made Jane this offer. Most thoughtful. Now, I'll just ring through to the office, to let Miss Clark know you're coming. And you will remember to apologize to Miss MacKenzie for missing her lacrosse game, won't you? Yes, of course you will.

"Jane! Are you just going to stand there with your mouth open, staring into space?"

"No, sorry, Miss Anthony. I'm sorry. Thank you," said Jane.

"I don't know what's the matter with you. You've been

17

getting more and more uncouth recently. I'm not the only one to have noticed it. Several members of staff have mentioned it to me."

"I'm sorry, Miss Anthony," said Jane.

Audrey refrained from laughing until the two girls were halfway between the drawing room and the school secretary's office.

"All right," said Jane, "very funny. But you don't know what *you* sounded like. He's really *pretty*, isn't he! Oh, Miss Anthony, thanks a *lot*! That's really *super*! So polite, my dear. So charming. So . . . so couth."

"Of course," said Audrey. "What else? Just because you've got no more idea of charm than a female buffalo. Come on, Plain Face, are you going to ring first, or me?"

"You," said Jane.

Now that they'd reached the school office, now that the red-faced, bespectacled secretary was pushing the telephone towards them across her desk, she felt, once more closing in on her, the darkness of panic, of loss of control that'd frightened her earlier in the basement. Her mouth began to dry out, as she watched the casual way in which Audrey hoisted one buttock onto a radiator, stretched to pick up a pencil, dialed, with the pencil's end, her London number, then clamped the receiver between her shoulder and chin, so that her lips were stretched open and her eyes became large and surprised. She looked so competent, as though she spent her life ringing people. Whereas, for Jane, the telephone was an instrument of torture.

If it rang when she was at home, she would wait for someone else to answer it; or, no one else being there, she would walk slowly, slowly, towards the hall of the large, old house, holding her breath and willing the bell to stop of its own accord.

The mechanical pings and whirs; the disembodied voice; the distorted phrases that she had either to pretend to have understood, or, worse humiliation, to ask to have repeated; the panic of having to make decisions without the time to think, all these made her mouth dry out, her palms sweat and her neck erupt in a pink and mottled rash.

It was ridiculous, she knew. Girls of her age were supposed to like nothing more than talking on the telephone. Audrey and her other friends did like nothing more, would slip away from the school as often as possible to call boyfriends, parents, anyone, from a coin box in the nearest village. But Jane couldn't help it, she *hated* it. And today, in particular, the thought of having to speak with her father, of being forced to reopen the . . .

"Plain! I said it's okay. It's fine. My mama would be delighted to have you to stay. She doesn't know what she's letting herself in for, of course, but still . . . Now, go on, you get it fixed up at your end."

"Have you *finished*?" asked Jane.

"Yes, of course. For goodness' sake, didn't you hear me? Now, go on."

"Will you dial for me?"

"What? What on earth for?"

"Nothing. I just . . . Nobody may even be at home."

"Why not? Your papa works from home, doesn't he?"

"Yes," said Jane.

She tried to imagine him, her father, hunched over his typewriter with his fingers poised in midair. She tried to

19

imagine his book-lined study, his desk, the two sash windows in front of which his desk was placed and through which he would sometimes stare for minutes on end, blind to the garden, the boxwood hedge, the fields, the sky, deaf to his family's calling. She tried to imagine the large, sunlit house as it must be when she wasn't there: its doors flung open, its corridors alive with shouts and running footsteps, its rooms sweet with the smell of cut flowers and animated by a confusion of discarded boots and coats, of half-finished sewing, of toys, the dog's bone and the kite that her father was going to mend as soon as he had the time.

She closed her eyes. She inhaled.

She walked to the desk. She lifted the receiver and listened for the right humming sound. Then she dialed.

"Daddy?"

"Hello? Who's that?"

"It's me, Daddy. It's Jane."

"Jane!"

The voice deepened, opened out, until it had found the suitable note for greeting an oldest daughter.

"Jane! But where can you be ringing from? Don't tell me you've run away from school."

"Of course not," she said, glad that only she could hear his end of the conversation, although Audrey might have thought it witty.

She said, "I got your letter."

"Good. Good."

"The one about Mummy and the baby," she said.

"Ah, yes, now you're not worrying about that, are you? I did say you weren't to. Everything's quite under control, darling. Your mama's pretty nearly her old self again and the little Diggory seems to get bigger every second. He'll be bursting out of his glass case before long."

"Diggory?"

"Ah! Yes. I'm afraid so. Your mother assures me it means 'an exposed child.' I've told her that the only thing he'll be exposed to'll be a lot of teasing, but she's implacable. Immovable. You know how she gets."

"It's a boy then," said Jane. "You didn't say, in the letter."

"Didn't I?"

There was a silence. Jane focused on the black, plastic cup in front of her mouth, on the concentric rings of holes in the cup's base, around which dust had gathered. All that she *wanted* to say was "Can I go out with a friend next weekend?" All that she wanted her father to answer was either yes or no.

But the telephone, as she'd known it would, was confusing everything, was making everything muddled, unclean and dangerous.

She clenched her fingers, her forehead.

She said, "Anyway, it doesn't matter."

"No, that's right," said her father's voice. "Well, darling, what a lovely surprise hearing from you. Everything all right at your end? No terrible exams coming up?"

"There are, but they're not the really important ones. Those are next term."

"Good."

"Look, Daddy," she said, speaking fast now, realizing that she must speak fast in order to avoid the apologies, the explanations, the justifications that her father would otherwise feel that he had to produce.

21

"Look, Daddy, about me not coming home next weekend, like I was supposed to. It's okay. A friend of mine, Audrey Croft, the one whose mother told her you were the best thing in the Sunday papers, she's said I can go out with her. So you don't have to worry. And she lives in London, so it'll be fun. It's all right, isn't it?"

Through the office window, she could see a straggling procession of yellow-sweatered, red-kneed girls approaching down the drive from the games fields.

"Look, I'm going to have to go soon, Daddy. But it is all right, isn't it, about next weekend?"

"You're going out with a girl whose mother thinks I'm the best thing in the Sunday papers?"

"Yes. . . ."

"Well then, of course that's all right. A perfectly trustworthy woman, obviously."

"Yes. Right. Thanks, then."

Jane knew that there was something else she should say before she rang off, but she wanted only to get away, to get back inside the day that she could see, rolling on without her, through the glass of the office window.

"I'm going to have to go," she said again.

"Off you pop, then. Behave yourself. And we'll be seeing you at Easter, I expect."

"Yes. Well, 'bye, Daddy."

" 'Bye, darling."

" 'Bye."

As soon as she'd replaced the receiver, Jane swung towards Audrey and said, "Right, let's hurry, hey? Come on, Aug, let's hurry. Get our apologies to the Haggis over. Come on. Are you *coming*? Come on!"

3

"Plain, is it true then, about your mother? Is she *very* ill?"

"Aren't you worried? You must be desperately worried."

"Oh, for goodness' sake," said Jane, dropping her fork onto her plate, raising her eyes to the vaulted dining-room ceiling.

It was suppertime and all afternoon and evening it had been like this: the curious looks, the questions, the eager, greedy, sympathetic smiles. Why hadn't Audrey kept her mouth shut? Why had she found it necessary to inform everybody what had happened?

She said, "You're the biggest lot of morons going. Haven't you ever heard of a hyperbole?"

"What's that?"

"It's a figure of speech, idiot," said Nicky Lawrence, who was sitting opposite to Jane at the dining-room table. "Synonyms, metaphors, hyperboles. Figures of speech."

"Exactly," said Jane, picking up her fork again, poking at the baked beans on her plate. "It means an exaggeration. Like Augy making out my mama's on death's doorstep when all she's gone and done is had another baby. Really, you're all so gullible."

She picked up her glass and swallowed some water. She replaced the glass beside her plate.

"Isn't it true then?" asked Loretta van Straten, a frizz of blonde hair obscuring her Dresden-blue eyes, a chewed piece of sausage churning in her open mouth. "Wasn't the baby born early at all?"

Jane said, "Yes, of course, it's true. But babies are often born early. If you knew the first thing about anything, you'd know that."

"Just because *you're* a walking dictionary . . ."

"Oh Retta," said Nicky Lawrence. "Close your mouth, can't you? You're making me feel sick. Of course, Plain knows about babies. After all, her mother *is* the British record holder at having them."

She smiled, twisting her thin, pale lips into a sneer. Those close enough to her end of the table to hear her laughed. After a moment, Jane, too, laughed.

She said, "British record holder? *European* record holder, at *least*, my dear Nicky."

"I apologize. In fact, I'm almost certain she's world. Yes, she is, she's *world* champion."

"*Universe* champion," said Jane.

"*Galaxy* champion," said Nicky.

"*Infinity* champion," said Jane.

Nicky said, "In a word, in one word, unbeatable."

"Invincible."

"Supreme."

"The tops. The best. Super rabbit!" said Jane, tipping her chair onto its hind legs and smiling across the dining room at Audrey, who, fork poised halfway between plate and mouth, was glancing in her direction.

"Will you lot down the bottom end be a bit quieter?" said the prefect in charge of the table. "And stop rocking your chair, Jane Rackham. Do you want to be sent out?"

Jane dropped forward. The laughter at the table drained

24

away, ran down into the general froth of voices that bubbled and swirled around the tables, below the high, cold, empty vault of the dining-room ceiling.

"And you're not leaving all *that*," said the prefect, still talking to Jane. "I don't mind you leaving a bit, but not all that."

"I'm not hungry," said Jane.

She wasn't. Suddenly, she felt as she sometimes felt when she was very tired, as though her throat had closed up and her stomach was tied in a knot.

"Just have another mouthful, then spread it around a bit," said the prefect, who was one of the more tolerable ones, a sallow-skinned, bespectacled cellist and lead alto in the school choir.

"Really, Valery, I can't," said Jane.

Around them, at the other tables, plates, knives, forks and glasses were being piled up for collection by the maids.

Loretta van Straten gripped the edge of Jane's plate and said, "Give it to me. I'll eat it."

"You've already *had* two helpings," said the prefect.

"Let her, if she wants it," said Jane.

"What's the matter with you, Jane? Are you feeling ill?"

"No."

Then Mrs. Bailey, who, as duty-mistress, was supervising supper from the top table, rang the handbell and called out, "Silence! Silence girls! Now, will you all hurry up and clear away, or we'll be late for chapel."

Jane looked at the prefect, trying not to plead, trying to let no emotion escape through her eyes or her mouth.

The prefect shrugged.

With the dexterity of a practiced pickpocket, Loretta

van Straten slid Jane's plate onto hers and began to devour the remaining sausages and beans, while, all about her, crockery and cutlery clanked together, glasses were stacked into towers, napkins were folded and supper came to its end.

4

Supper, chapel, free time, then bed. By ten o'clock, on that Tuesday evening, the last dormitory light had been extinguished, the last *rat-tat* of slippered feet had faded into silence along the upper corridors of the school and the last door had banged shut.

Beyond the windows of the slumbering house, rain no longer fell. A moon like a toenail paring floated against a clear sky, surrounded by hard, white stars. Purple trees trembled against the comparative light of the skyline. A fox barked.

At least, Jane *supposed* that it was a fox. It wasn't a dog, anyway, not with that rasp to its voice. She pressed her face against the glass of her dormitory window and stared into the semidarkness of the night, hoping to see some animal movement emerge from the ferns and thick undergrowth that bordered the school grounds. None came. Only vegetation rustled and shifted, uneasy in a dying wind.

Tired of staring, Jane closed her eyes. The cold of the glass was gentle against her forehead.

Behind her, Loretta van Straten and her best friend, Rose Mercer, were whispering together. Sharing chocolate, Jane supposed, from the crackle of foil, the suppressed giggles, the sudden, satisfied silences.

Loretta, like a cow, ate continuously. Whether in chapel, in class, or on the games field, her round, pink cheeks were invariably swollen by the lump of a boiled sweet, the pulpy remains of a biscuit. Her lips seemed always to be dusted with sugar. Her thick, golden hair spun away from her head like candy floss.

Rose, on the other hand, was sallow and skinny and dark. The only effect that they had on her, the sweetmeats that she was forced to devour as the price of her friendship with Loretta, was to crowd the crease of her chin, and the creases on either side of her long, sharp nose, with spots. Her forehead, too, was always erupting in whiteheads. Jane disliked her.

The only other member of the dormitory, Ruth Bottomly, puffed and grunted beneath her bedclothes, suffocating in the cause of literature. Already this term she'd read the whole of Tolstoy's *Anna Karenina* by flashlight, and was now well into volume two of his *War and Peace*.

Ruth, Rose and Loretta. All in all, Jane's wasn't an attractive dormitory. Audrey, sharing with Nicky Lawrence, Miranda Spurling and Simone de Preville, had had much better luck than she this year.

Jane opened her eyes and tightened the cord of her dressing gown until it bit into her waist. Her toes were blue, curled on the linoleum. She clenched them, then released them. She considered climbing back into her bed.

Earlier in the evening, she'd thought that she was so tired that she would fall asleep the moment lights were out. She'd looked forward to it, to the tightness of sheets and blankets beneath her chin, to the comfort of knees pressed up to the chest and arms encircling a flimsy feather pillow.

Now, she no longer felt tired. Or rather, she felt exhausted, but couldn't sleep. Every time that she closed her eyes, the inside of her head would fill with a hiss and whisper of ugly, questioning voices, of horrible shadows, of fear. But why?

The drama was over. The sensation of her father's letter had played itself out, even before the bell had been rung for bedtime. By then, in the fifth-form classroom, they'd been discussing the games mistress's boyfriend and whether the fact that he hadn't been seen for a couple of weeks meant that he'd finally got close enough to the Haggis to discover her halitosis. Yes, the letter had long been forgotten.

Nor was there any reason why it should not have been, why Jane should keep on remembering it. Why *did* she? Her mother was all right. The baby was all right. Everyone else was all right. There was nothing more to be thought about. Was there?

Staring hard into the moon-silvered, wind-rustling night, Jane forced herself to concentrate on something new: on how good it would be to spend the weekend in London with Audrey, staying in Audrey's Kensington flat, visiting the shops, the cinema maybe, a restaurant. She tried to remember exactly what Mrs. Croft looked like, what color her eyes were, how her voice sounded. She tried to remember whether Henrietta, Audrey's sister, was married. She'd a feeling that she was, but it might just have been a boyfriend that Audrey'd talked about. Or was she thinking of someone else altogether?

Suddenly, Jane couldn't think anymore. Her head

snapped upright and she realized that she'd fallen asleep. She stretched her eyes, refocusing on the dappled slope of the school lawn, on the blackness where lawn merged into undergrowth.

Then she listened.

No sound came from the room behind her.

She turned. Immediately beside where she was standing, Ruth Bottomly's large, red face lay displayed in the center of a pillow, eyes closed, mouth open, breath wheezing in and out between cracked, mustachioed lips.

On the other side of the dormitory, Rose and Loretta also appeared to be sleeping. Their beds were motionless. Loretta's floral eiderdown had fallen into a mound on the floor beside her.

Jane tiptoed back through the room, took off her dressing gown, draped it across the back of her bedside chair and rolled between cold sheets into sleep.

She didn't hear the chapel clock strike eleven. Nor did she hear it strike twelve, one, two. Nor did she see the dawn seep upwards into the night, like a wash of pink watercolor over the dark mass of treetops on the eastern horizon.

Part 2

5

To the left, to the right, to the left lurched the train, gathering speed as the last stop before London was left behind. Jane and Audrey, locked in one of the train's lavatories, grabbed at each other's coat sleeve for balance. In the soap-spattered looking glass over the lavatory basin, their twin reflections shook; then steadied; steadied; settled; began once more to peer back at them, as the train relaxed into its new, easy momentum.

"Oh, Lord," said Jane, seeing her face once more.

For the last quarter of an hour, she and Audrey had been putting on their makeup. She might as well not have bothered.

"*Look* at me."

London was only minutes away and still they were undisguised: the pink, L-shaped scar in her left eyebrow that she'd got from falling off a bicycle two summer holidays previously; the hooked bulb of her nose that made her look, so her father said, like a blonde Turk; the enormity of her

33

mouth. She'd tried to do *something* with them, had glossed her lips and darkened her eyebrows and spiked her lashes slate-gray; but to no avail.

"I look *aw*ful."

"Oh, shut up," said Audrey.

"But I do."

"Look at *me*, then."

Jane obeyed, but not for long. Audrey, as she had known she would, looked wonderful; not just beautiful, but sophisticated, adult, in control. Jane's stomach tightened with a mixture of envy, admiration and fear.

Fear?

Fear of *what*? Of being away from the school? Of being alone with Audrey, away from the protection of school?

No, that didn't make sense. She was *glad* to be going out. She forced her stomach to relax its knotted grip.

At that moment, down the train corridor, came the sound of a shrill, Scottish voice calling, "Jane! Audrey! What on *earth* are you doing in there? Not painting your faces, I hope. If you are, you know that I'll have to report you to Miss Anthony."

"Oh, shut up Haggis," whispered Audrey. "Stupid, bloody cow."

And Jane's stomach tightened again, almost as though the insult had been aimed at her.

But Audrey was *glad* to have her, or she wouldn't have asked her in the first place, would she? And Mrs. Croft was going to be there to meet them at the station. She was going to take them, in a taxi, back to the flat. Jane'd see Audrey's room, Audrey's clothes, Audrey's stereo. It was going to be fun. She knew it.

"Come *on*."

"What?"

"Come *on*," said Audrey. "Open the door. You're ready, aren't you? Or were you planning on spending the whole weekend in here?"

"What? Oh," said Jane. "Oh, you don't like it? I thought it was quite congenial. Hot and cold running water . . ."

"Open the door."

"Perhaps you're right. There isn't much of a view."

But still she paused. Suddenly, she wanted to ask, "Augy, you don't regret having invited me out with you, do you?"

Knowing, however, that she mustn't, that, if she did, she would only make Audrey angrier, she smiled instead.

"Right then," she said. "Off we go. Have you got everything? Right."

Out over the river plunged the train, its wheels hammering the iron floor of the bridge, its flanks whipped by sunlight flashing through gaps in the crisscross metalwork that rose up on either side of it.

Into the dark of the station it gasped and juddered, dragging itself along by the platform, wheezing, slowly, slowly to a halt.

"All right, girls!" called Miss MacKenzie and spread herself out to block their exit through the carriage doorway.

She counted heads. She checked the luggage racks for forgotten overnight cases. She ordered Beverly Matterson, from the first form, to straighten her socks. She reminded Audrey Croft and Jane Rackham that she was going to report them to the headmistress for insolent disobedience. She distributed tickets.

"Don't push along the corridor," she called. "Be careful

35

stepping down. Don't fall onto the rails. Stay with me, girls. Stay with *me*."

But already Audrey and Jane were lost from Miss Mac-Kenzie, swept away from her by the tide of people rushing along the platform towards the ticket barrier. They could hear her voice, still, shrill above the loudspeaker announcements and the clanging of carriage doors, but they could no longer see her. They passed the ticket barrier. In the bustling, glass-roofed station hall, beside a timetable board, Audrey came to a halt.

Jane said, "Is this where she usually meets you, your mama?"

Still screaming, Miss MacKenzie cantered past them. Her horselike face, as mottled and pink as an overripe strawberry, clashed with the orange of her hair. Surrounded by other people, real people, she looked even more absurd than she did at school, and Jane felt a moment's shame for the woman, a moment's embarrassment that she should be so exposed. Then she turned away from her, back towards Audrey.

"Can you see her yet?" she asked. "Your mama. Is she . . . ?"

"Look, will you *stop* it? Will you just stop whining and going *on* at me?"

"I wasn't," said Jane. "I just . . ."

She shrugged her shoulders.

"Okay. But what's up with you, Augy? Why've you gone so niggly?"

"I haven't gone niggly. It's *you*. You're beginning to get up my nose, if you really want to know."

"Well, I'm sorry," said Jane, shrugging once more, look-

36

ing at Audrey's profile and seeing how pinched her lips were, how tight the skin beside lipstick-scarlet mouth.

The fear that she'd felt in the train lavatory, the need to ask whether Audrey really wanted her there, returned. In a flash of panic, she raked, with her eyes, the crowd in the station hall, but Miss MacKenzie had gone. The other girls had gone. There was no one there who knew her, or whom she knew.

She licked her lips. She looked down at her coat, at her stockinged legs, at the toes of her gray leather shoes.

It'll be all right as soon as Mrs. Croft arrives, she told herself.

She was, however, no longer certain that this was true.

There'd been something in Audrey's face, in the *tightness* of Audrey's face, in the tightness of Audrey's voice when she'd said, as though from a long way away, "You're beginning to get up my nose," that was different from her usual, school ill temper. It was older than that. It was larger than that. It was frightening.

6

"Audrey! Baby! Darling! Have I kept you waiting *ages*?"

She arrived. In a flurry of jasmine scent and chiffon scarves and long, waving arms; gasping for lack of breath; ten minutes late; Mrs. Croft arrived.

"The wretched taxi came *quite* the longest way here. I very nearly didn't tip him, the brute. Are you *furious* with me? I bet you are. Let me *see* you, darling. Oh, it feels as though I haven't seen you for years. What've you got on your face? Never mind! You're here, that's the important thing. And aren't you even going to kiss me?"

Stunned, relieved, delighted, Jane watched as mother and daughter kissed one another, as Mrs. Croft grabbed Audrey to her and covered her face with kisses.

"Oh, darling, I've been rushing about all *morning*, getting things ready for you. I thought I'd *never* get away in time. And then, when I did, that villainous taxi! I could've *cried*, baby."

Her voice, like a flock of excited birds, swooped around them. Her flourishing arms enmeshed them. Mesmerized, Jane couldn't begin to remember of what it was she'd been frightened one minute before.

Frightened? She must have been mad. She must've been nervous, or something stupid like that.

"And is this Jane? Hello, Jane. It's *lovely* that you've been able to come out with Audrey. I've heard so much about you, in Audrey's letters, of course. Oh, I see *you*'ve been painting your face, too. Don't you think . . . ? No, of course not. You're so pretty it doesn't really matter *what* you do. How lovely to be young!

"And how's your mother, Jane? What a terrible thing! But I'm sure it'll all be fine. And your father? Working dreadfully hard, I expect, to put food into all those hungry little mouths. He *is* a charming man. And deliciously, wickedly funny. I met him at Speech Day last year. You will send him my regards when you write to him next, won't you? He probably won't remember me. We shared a joke about a misquotation from Pope that your headmistress made, during one of those interminable speeches. See if he remembers *that*."

"Did you?" asked Jane, laughing. "What was it? What did the Termite say wrong?"

"Now I expect you're both . . . What?" asked Mrs. Croft. "I'm sorry, Jane darling, what did you say? Are those your cases? Let me take one of them. We'd better rush, or we'll absolutely *never* get another taxi. It took me half an hour to find the wretched man who brought me here."

"Look, Mummy . . ." said Audrey.

Still laughing, Jane said, "Mrs. Croft! What was it the Ter . . . I mean Miss Anthony got wrong?"

"Oh, I don't think you'd understand, Jane. You'd have to know the original lines to understand the joke."

"But I probably . . ."

"*Look*, Mummy," said Audrey.

And Jane froze.

For it hadn't gone. It was still there: the tightness, the hardness, the inexplicable anger in Audrey's voice.

"*Look*, Mummy! Will you listen? I thought *you* might take the cases home and Plain and I'd come on later. We want to do a bit of shopping and so on. *You* know. Probably have lunch in a hamburger place, or a pizza place, I don't know. Anyway . . . Anyway, okay?"

The laughter dead in her stomach, Jane waited, waited for Mrs. Croft's reaction, knowing, however, by the tightness that was closing her throat, what it would be.

Slowly, Audrey's mother lowered to the ground the overnight case that she'd picked up. Her high forehead, beneath its sweep of gray-streaked hair, contracted into a bunch of vertical furrows. Her large, green eyes became triangular.

"Baby," she said and her voice was unsteady. "Baby, I've made you a special lunch."

"I expect it's only salads and things, though, isn't it?"

"Yes! Coleslaw and eggs mayonnaise and that delicious smoked sausage from the delicatessen."

"Well, it'll keep then."

"But it's your *favorite*. Do *you* like smoked sausage, Jane? Or maybe you've never tasted it. This one's particularly special. Audrey and I both love it. Don't we, darling?"

Jane was glad that Mrs. Croft wasn't really talking to her. She shifted her gaze to the far end of the station hall, so as not to see, so as not to hear, if it were possible, the conversation that was taking place beside her.

Why was Audrey being so hard, so vicious? And why was Mrs. Croft not fighting back? Couldn't she just have said, "Behave yourself. You'll do as you're told"? Or laughed the whole thing off, if she'd wanted? Or . . . anything! Anything other than this: to wheedle and plead and beg, of her own *daughter.*

What was *wrong* with them?

Audrey was saying, "For goodness' sake, woman, stop going *on* about it."

Jane listened to the rumble of incoming trains, the squealing of brakes, the banging of doors, the shreds of murmured conversation that blew past her, that swept towards the exit way, towards the sunlight and the splashes of red from the sides of passing buses and the soft pounding of a pneumatic drill.

"Jane, darling, *you* tell me. You're not as horrid as my little daughter there. Which would *you* prefer? Some delicious salads that I bought especially for you, or an expensive, unnourishing hamburger? You can go out again as soon as you've eaten."

Mrs. Croft swung back to face Audrey before she'd even finished addressing Jane.

"I *really* don't see what the problem is, darling. You can have lunch with me and go out shopping as soon as you've finished. I thought you liked the shops around us *best*, in any case."

"Mummy, look, we'll eat the damn salad tomorrow. Okay?"

"Sweetheart, why are you *doing* this?"

Jane didn't know why, either. She didn't want to know. She wanted only to be out in the sunlight, to be out in the street that pounded and roared, that glittered and shone through the arch of the exit way. So that when Audrey pushed her arm and said, "We'll see you this evening then. Okay? Come on. Come on, Plain, move," she went without turning around, without saying thanks, or good-bye; with nothing in her head at all.

7

"So! Fantastic, hey? Freedom at last," said Audrey, tossing the fringe from her forehead, plunging her legs beneath the seat in front of theirs, flexing and relaxing her toes.

"Look out, London, we're coming," she said, then sighed as though with supreme contentment and crossed her arms behind her head.

They were on the top deck of a bus traveling north up the Charing Cross Road. Below them, men and women hurried along the sunlit pavement, some carrying parcels, some briefcases, one, an old man in brown overalls, a tower of paper cups with lids on.

"You know the first thing I'm going to do?" asked Audrey. "When we reach Oxford Street? I'm going to buy myself something. Something . . . Well, it doesn't matter. You'll see. What about you, Plain? Are you going to get anything?"

"I don't know," said Jane.

"Come on. There must be something."

"I don't *know*."

Audrey parted her lips as though to speak again, then closed them. She tipped her face towards the bus's yellow ceiling and gently closed her eyes.

Jane stared at her.

It was incredible. The meeting with Mrs. Croft, the tension, the anger, the pleading and the rejection might none of it ever have happened.

Maybe it hadn't happened. Maybe Jane had imagined it, or given it too much importance.

No, she hadn't. She knew she hadn't.

Without meaning to, Jane shivered. She looked away from Audrey and down, through sun-streaked, dirt-smeared glass, to the street along which they were crawling. She saw the words *"I laughed till I cried"* in large, black letters on a billboard outside a theater. She saw a dog sit waiting in front of a music-shop door.

No! No, she *must*'ve imagined it. How could anything

terrible, anything dangerous have taken place between Audrey and Audrey's mother, ten minutes ago, in the station hall?

It hadn't. Jane swung away from the window, from the jostle and glare of the street, to the body stretched out beside her on the seat of the bus. Audrey's eyes were still closed, her face still relaxed, her lips still gently smiling.

"Anyway," said Jane, then stopped and inhaled, her voice having sounded too loud, too urgent, too frantic.

"Anyway," she said again, "I haven't got much money."

"What are you talking about?" said Audrey at last.

"To buy things. I haven't got that much money."

"You've got enough for lunch, I hope."

"Oh, yes. Yes, of course, I didn't mean *that*. I just . . . Anyway, what is it? That *you're* going to buy?"

"Never you mind."

"Go on. Tell me."

"You'll see."

"Is it fantastic?"

Audrey opened her eyes. She looked at Jane and, lips squeezed together, elongated her smile.

At once, Jane smiled back.

"Okay. Well, I'll know soon, anyway, won't I? And then what? Then we'll go and get a hamburger, shall we?"

"No, I thought something better than that," said Audrey.

"What?"

"A pub. How about going to a pub for lunch?"

"But . . . But we can't, can we? We're not old enough."

"Who's to know? So long as you don't go all red and

43

stupid when they ask you what you want to drink. Go on. Go on, Plain. What'll you say?"

"What d'you mean?"

"When they *ask* you."

"Er . . . I don't know. Gin!"

"Gin and what?"

"Tonic. Yes, tonic."

"Have you ever *drunk* gin?"

"Yes! For goodness' sake! Of course I have."

"What does it taste like, then?"

"Like *gin*. What else do you think? No, actually, it doesn't. It tastes like tonic, if you put enough in. So there, Snot Face. I'm not *quite* moronic, you know."

"Aren't you?" asked Audrey, laughing, flinging her gaze like a light, easy net around the bus's interior.

"No," said Jane, laughing too.

"Hey," said Audrey, shifting suddenly closer to Jane, turning and approaching her mouth to Jane's ear. "Don't look, but there's a guy up at the front giving us some pretty hot looks. D'you see him?"

"Where?"

"Don't *stare*. Look, there, there, just buying his ticket now. See, I told you! He's dropped all his money he's so excited."

"Him?"

"Well, all right, so he's two feet tall and got acne. But just wait till we *really* get started."

She laughed again and, again, Jane laughed with her.

Then, without warning, as though something had snapped inside her, Jane felt the laughter rip from her control. Like an earthquake, it shook her, battered her, choked her, so that she had to bury her face in the back of the rough red seat and gasp for air.

"Behave yourself, woman," she heard Audrey say.

"I can't help it."

"I didn't say anything *that* funny."

"I know. I know."

"Then pull yourself together. People are staring at us. Plain! Pull yourself together. You're embarrassing me."

"I'm *happy*."

"Well . . . Well, *that* makes a change, anyway."

"I know. Hey! Aug!"

The laughter was subsiding, but the relief, the joy still sang inside Jane's head.

"Aug, after we've been to the pub, *then* what?"

"Are you sure you've quite recovered?"

"Yes. Yes. *Then* what, Aug? What're we going to do this afternoon?"

Jane asked, but the answer was unimportant. All that mattered was that Audrey knew what it was.

"Plain Face, *move* it for goodness' sake. This is our stop."

All that mattered was that Audrey was in control. The scene in the station hall with Mrs. Croft, the earlier quarrel with the Haggis: both these were swept to one side, as Jane stumbled after Audrey down the narrow stairs of the bus, as she leaped with Audrey to the pavement, as she ran to catch up with the green of Audrey's coat, before it disappeared in the kaleidoscopic Oxford Street crowd.

8

By half past two that afternoon, the March sun was beginning to lose its heat. Still bright, it sparkled along the rim of Jane's half-closed eyelashes, as she lay on her back on the slatted, wooden park bench; but she had to grope for her coat buttons, nonetheless, and heave them around to meet the row of corresponding holes.

"Stop fidgeting, will you?" said Audrey, who was lying on the bench beside her, her face next to Jane's crossed ankles, her crossed ankles next to Jane's face. "Do you want to give me a black eye or something?"

"I'm getting cold," said Jane.

"You've always got to have *some* sort of problem, haven't you?"

Jane said, "Is your head still spinning?"

They'd had two gins each for lunch; two gins and only a packet of crisps between them, as the pub into which they'd gone hadn't been one that served food. To begin with, Jane had thought that the drink wasn't having an effect on her and had been half-proud, half-disappointed.

"I think I'm immune to alcohol," she'd said, leaning across the small, round corner table at which Audrey and she had been sitting.

"You should have a look at your face, then," had said Audrey.

"Why? What's the matter with it?"

"It's bright red."

She'd clapped against her cheeks the palm of her hands. Either her face was very hot, or her hands were very cold. She'd wondered which.

"Go to the loo and have a look at yourself," had said Audrey.

"Okay."

It had been on standing up, or, rather, on attempting to stand up, that she'd realized that she *must* be drunk. In any case, her sense of balance had deserted her and her sense of distance. Reaching for her bag, she'd knocked an empty glass from the table, had watched it topple slowly, slowly towards the carpet, had been unable to move to catch it.

"Did you see that?" she'd asked.

"Me and everybody else. Go on, Fain Place, go and tidy yourself up, so we can leave."

"Fain Place! Did you hear what you called me? Fain Place! You're pisseder than I am, Augy."

"For goodness' sake, don't laugh like that. We'll get arrested."

In the ladies' lavatory, she'd bumped into her face on the back of a closed door. It had grinned at her, beamed at her, large, wild and flushed in the circle of yellowing glass. Her eyes had been enormous.

"Hello," she'd said.

She'd thought that she was beautiful.

And still she felt beautiful, lying on her back on the slatted, wooden park bench, the fingers of her right hand tickled by grass blades, the sunlight explosive on the tips of her half-closed eyelashes, the inside of her head soaring and swooping. She felt invincible, omnipotent, peaceful, in spite of the cool wind that was begin-

47

ning to ruffle her face and her hands. She felt happy.

"My head's like the sea," she said. "Whoom, crashing in. Shooh, dragging out. Whoom, in. Shooh, out. Whoom . . ."

"Don't keep on *talking* about it," said Audrey.

"Why not? It's a lovely feeling. Like having a giant shell, instead of a brain. You know, one of those shells they make you listen to when you're a kid, to hear the tide. *You* know."

"I don't know and I don't want to know. Just shut up, will you? I think I'm going to be sick."

Forcing her swollen eyelids apart, Jane eased herself onto her elbows. Above her, the sun was being drawn behind a curtain of dark-gray cloud and, to her right, across the grass, across the gravel paths of the park, across the empty, flapping deck chairs and the benches, a swift, silent shadow was spreading.

"*Now* what's the matter?" asked Audrey.

Jane looked at her.

"Are you really going to be sick?" she asked.

"Probably. What on earth did you make me eat those disgusting crisps for? They were as stale as old socks. Oh, God, I keep tasting them in the back of my throat. Can't you?"

Audrey was lying on the inside of the bench, her body half tipped towards Jane's and wedged in by it. Her eyes were closed, her mouth was ajar. A short, deep furrow drew her brows together. Her praying hands formed a pillow beneath her left cheek.

"Say something," she said.

"What?" asked Jane.

"Anything. Just keep talking."

"Okay. I know. Can I see the bracelet again? Will you let me?" asked Jane.

Audrey eased one hand from the triangular vise formed by the bench seat, her face and Jane's right foot and raised it into the air. A sliver of silver links ran down her arm from her wrist, caught on the cuff of her coat sleeve, hung there, swung there, glinted and flashed deep amber.

"All right?" she asked.

"Please," said Jane.

Levering the top half of her body upright, she swung her legs and feet off the bench until she was sitting perched beside Audrey's supine body. Then she reached up to touch the bracelet. She drew it down into her lap. Audrey's fingers uncurled as they landed against her thighs.

"It's the most wonderful thing I've ever seen," she said. "It really is, Augy."

It was an "identity" bracelet, but not an ordinary, cheap one, such as everyone'd had a few years before. Each link of *this* bracelet was a heavy, hexagonal oblong of sterling silver, scooped and flattened on four of its sides to lie smoothly beneath, and above, its neighbors, slotting in with them so well as to give the impression of being not just bits joined together, but a flowing, organic, continuous run of light. The nameplate, too, was solid, and curved to fit flush against the wrist.

"You won't find another one like that," had said the man in the shop where Audrey had taken Jane on getting down from the bus. "Handmade, that is, dear," he'd said.

"I know," had said Audrey.

It appeared that she'd coveted it since the Christmas holidays.

"But where did you get all the money from?" had asked Jane.

"Where do you think? From my mother, of course. I've just got to ask her for a couple of *shillings* and she's cramming pound notes in my purse. When I asked her for *this*, though . . . I asked her for it last Christmas. She'd *said* anything I wanted. But . . . Oh, she said it was vulgar and unfeminine, just a passing fad and she'd rather get me something in gold. What she *meant* was, *she*'d rather choose what I had. Just so she could feel . . . Oh, forget it. It doesn't matter. I've got it, so . . ."

"I prefer silver to gold, anyway," said Jane, now, stroking her hand backwards and forwards between the twin smoothnesses of the chain and the inside of Audrey's wrist. "It's cleaner, somehow. You know. Like Greek temples as opposed to Italian churches. And have you felt? Where it's been against your skin, it's quite warm. But the outside's as cold as . . ."

"Um, nice," said Audrey. "Go on doing that."

"What?"

"Tickling my wrist like that. It's nice."

Audrey's eyes were still closed, but the furrow had disappeared from between her brows and her lips were spread in a smile. Her face, a quarter turned into the seat of the bench, was heavy with relaxation. The collars of her coat and of her dress were turned back to reveal a strong, white neck and, creeping underneath the chin, a secret network of delicate, pale-blue veins.

She looked lovely and sleek and contented, like one of Miss Anthony's cats when it rolled onto its back, retracted its legs and exposed, for stroking, the warm, thick downiness of its stomach. Yet touch that stomach too roughly, or even, sometimes, as gently as you might, with what speed could those front and back claws slash together to tear your hand, with what indignation could the cat jump back to its feet, could it snarl, sneer and stride away to the far side of the Termite's drawing room.

"Why've you stopped?" asked Audrey. "Go on."

Jane braced her fingers. Around them, the grass was becoming agitated. A double sheet of newspaper somersaulted over the path beside the bench, then hit the base of a tree and stuck there, beating to be free. Two women hurried past, one of them wheeling a stroller and, as she walked, leaning forward to tug the stroller's hood up and over the head of a sleeping child. Close behind the women, a man came by, his head sunk into his shoulders, his hands sunk into the pockets of his beltless, overlarge raincoat.

"Go on," said Audrey.

Jane began again to move the tips of her fingers, stroking them backwards and forwards, around and around, confined between the hard, warm metal and the soft, warm hillock that was the inside of Audrey's wrist.

"Nice," said Audrey.

She turned her face away from the bench seat, towards Jane. She half opened her eyes.

"What's the matter, Plain Face?"

"Nothing," said Jane.

"Are you frightened people are going to think we're a pair of old lesbians?"

51

Jane's hand wriggled free, sprung back, formed itself into a fist against her waist.

"Great!" she said.

Audrey laughed.

"Come *on*. It wasn't *funny.* What d'you . . . ?"

"Look at you," said Audrey. "Old tight-lips Plain Face! Don't be such a prude. Such things exist, you know."

"I *know* that. I'm not *naive.* So why did you ask me to do it, then?"

"Because it was *nice.* "

Audrey pushed herself in to a kneeling position on the bench seat.

"For goodness' sake," she said, "it was a joke. You always take things so damn seriously. Why do you always have to go and spoil things?"

"*Me*? Why do *I* always have to go and spoil things?"

But Jane could hear the panic interwoven with her righteous indignation, the dread that Audrey might be right, that it might've been *her*, some fault of *hers* that had ruined the peace between them. She forced herself to relax, to unclench her fist.

Audrey said, "You oughtn't ever to sober up, you know that? Somebody ought to be paid to constantly top you up with gin. You were quite pleasant, when you were pissed."

"Well, *you* were quite disgusting," said Jane and watched as the anger withdrew from Audrey's face, as the amusement crept back.

"Didn't anyone ever teach you to hold your drink?" she asked.

"Listen to you!" said Audrey. "Who's talking? Knocking glasses off the table . . ."

"At least I wasn't sick all over the place."

"Nor was I."

"Jolly nearly."

"That was the crisps, Snot Face!"

"Liar!" said Jane, laughing too, feeling the tension of a minute before resolve itself into energy.

She jumped up. She clapped together her hands.

She said, "Well, what're we going to do now? Hey, Aug, what's next? Didn't you say you wanted to go to the movies?"

"Yes. Okay. But what's the rush? What time is it?"

Jane looked around. There was no clock; only the scurrying of papers and large, dry, toneless leaves across the grass; only a dog with flattened ears trotting towards the park exit.

"I don't know," she said, "but it's about to pour with rain, anyway. Come on. You don't want to get soaked, do you? Race you to the gate."

"We're not at school," said Audrey, settling back onto her haunches, opening her bag and extracting a looking glass. "Oh, my goodness, I look terrible. Why didn't you tell me?"

"You look fine," said Jane, restlessness leaping within her. Where it had come from, this feeling, she wasn't sure. She only knew that she wanted to move; move away from the shadows that troubled and darkened the grass; move away from the danger, of something, that chilled the afternoon air.

She jiggled her feet, her legs, the hands within the

pockets of her coat; while Audrey frowned, licked one fingertip and drew it along the grain of her eyebrows, arching them. It was absurd, Jane knew, but she had the feeling that Audrey was escaping from her into her own reflection. And there was nothing that she could do to stop it. She couldn't say "Hurry. I'm going." It was Audrey who knew where the cinema was and at what time the film began. It was Audrey's town, Audrey's day, and Jane *wanted* it to be like that. So, impotent, frustrated, unable to understand her impatience, she could only stand there, fists clenched, and wait.

Then, at last, they were off. They were going. They were going to the cinema. Audrey and she were going to the cinema, to see a film about which everyone at school had been talking for months, which everyone wanted to see. Now, Audrey and she were going to see it together.

Jane's hands unclenched within the pockets of her coat as they moved towards the park gate. She could no longer remember why it was that she'd clenched them in the first place; what fear, or stupid anxiety, it had been that had clamped them. She must've been mad.

"For goodness' sake, Plain, slow down. What's the matter with you?"

"It's going to *piss* any second, you imbecile, that's what."

"Okay, but I'm not about to break an ankle just because of that."

"You shouldn't wear such high heels, then, if you don't know how to walk in them."

"At least I don't stick out my bum when I walk."

"Oh! Who's so elegant and sophisticated?"

"Who's just a thick country bumpkin? No, *this* way, you

idiot. Don't you even know which way the bus stop is? Hey! Hurry! Come on! There's one coming."

"Okay," said Jane, breathless from movement, from laughter. "Don't flap. We'll get it. Go on. I'm just behind you."

9

"I still don't see why they had to make it X-rated," said Jane, as, three hours later, they stepped out of the cinema and into the evening street.

It was half past seven. The cars that sped past them threw ribbons of red-and-yellow light in their wake now. Now, too, the streetlamps were lit, their brash glow cutting the city off from the delicate sky, the pale, young moon; compelling attention down towards shop windows, the pavement, the gutter, where sodden rubbish lay hunched in sullen piles. Puddles burned with a dull, orange fever. Slapping shoes and spinning tires spat a ground mist of spray into the twilight.

"It wasn't *that* violent," said Jane.

Audrey asked, "Is that all you were interested in? The violence?"

"No. I just meant I don't see why it had to be an X. That's all."

"To keep stupid little twerps like *you* out," said Audrey.

They stood outside the large, glass cinema doors. The crowd emerging from the foyer behind them parted when it reached where they stood, then closed together again a few yards up the pavement; unaffected, like water.

Jane asked, "Why am I a twerp? What d'you mean? Do you think I didn't understand it or something?"

But Audrey only shrugged, as though, having left the cinema building, its warmth, its blue-smoke darkness, having stepped once more into the traffic-busy and pedestrian-scurrying street, some energy, some sense of direction had died in her.

Jane frowned. She began to say something.

Instead, she said, "Well, I *did* understand it, so there. And I liked it, too. Didn't you? Hey! Hey, they're going to be really jealous, aren't they, Nicky and Prevy and that lot, when they know we've seen it?"

But Audrey was no longer listening.

She'd half turned away from Jane, in the direction of the departing crowd, but her eyes weren't focused on that, either; were focused on nothing.

"What time is it?" she asked, and her voice was no less flat than the look in her eyes.

Jane held her breath.

Then, having allowed the air to escape in a slow stream from her lungs, she said, "I don't know. It must be about half past seven, I think. I think that's when the film was due to finish. Why?"

But she *knew* why. The day was over. Audrey's day, Audrey's day and hers, was finished. There was nowhere further to go, nothing more to do. The time had come to return to Mrs. Croft.

Inside her head, Jane heard herself say, "Look, why don't we go and have our supper somewhere around here? We never did have a hamburger, like we said we were going to." But Audrey was already moving away from her, was gliding, like a sleepwalker, along the edge of the pavement.

"Aug!"

"What's the *matter*? Just look for a taxi, will you? Keep your stupid eyes open. If we miss one in this weather, we'll never get another."

There was no way out. They were returning to Mrs. Croft. And wasn't that what Jane had wanted? Hadn't she *wanted* to see Audrey's home, to talk to her mother, to meet, perhaps, her sister and her sister's . . . Was it boyfriend, or husband?

Yes, no, *that* was right. Audrey's sister *was* married, to a man called Gary Somebody-or-other, who wrote plays. Jane remembered now. Oh, if only *they* could be there, this evening, then maybe . . . What?

"Come *on*, Plain, we're going to miss him."

A taxi had drawn to a halt a few yards in front of them. Spurred by the anger in Audrey's voice, Jane pushed through the crowd to reach it, to fumble with its door handle while Audrey gave her address, to open the door, to fall inside the warm body.

"Watch what you're doing with your feet, can't you? You nearly kicked me, you great oaf."

"Sorry," said Jane. "I didn't mean to."

Yes, if only Henrietta and her husband could be there, this evening.

But why? What did she suppose would be prevented by their presence? What did she think it was that might happen without them? Of what was she frightened?

Jane didn't know.

Only Audrey, sitting upright and tense beside her, her

right hand turning the silver bracelet around and around her left wrist, her eyes blank, as they stared through the back of the driver's head, through the wet glare of the night, towards Kensington: only Audrey knew.

Turning away from her friend, Jane touched her hair. She smoothed its sticky dampness against her head. She smoothed her skirt across her knees. Then, closing her legs together, sliding her feet a decorous distance to one side of her body, she watched the fare click up another unit on the meter.

Neither she spoke, nor Audrey spoke, until the taxi had drawn to a halt in a side street off Kensington High Street.

There, Jane followed Audrey down from the taxi to the pavement.

Twenty yards back, in the direction from which they had come, a thick, persistent stream of cars crept past the top of the street and, beyond the cars, glimpsed in between their close-packed bodies, a neon sign flashed on and off, advertising a jeans shop. Pedestrians also crossed at the top of the street, in ones and twos and bunches, but whatever sound these must have made, whatever sound the traffic must have made, was muted, here, into a soft, indefinite hum. It seemed to Jane as though she'd passed into another world, another plane of existence. She felt that, were she to try to run towards the end of the street, towards the cars, the people and the lights, she'd run forever without reaching them.

Beside her stood a mailbox. She touched it with her fingers. Beside the mailbox was a sapling, its trunk pushing up from a space between the paving stones, its thin branches displaying their blossom, colorless in the dusk. Other, similar, young trees were planted at intervals along the pavement, on either side of the street, and, behind them, on either side of the street, loomed the stern, silent facades of identical red-brick buildings, their windows for the most part dark, although one or two were slashed by yellow scars between badly drawn curtains.

Jane turned her face and looked at the particular entranceway in front of which they had stopped: a short flight of stone steps leading up to heavy, closed doors; the inscription "Flats G to L," in paint, on a fanlight above the doors; a vertical row of brass bell pushes to the right of the doors and a vertical row of small brass frames, holding cards with writing on them. The whole seemed designed not to let people out or in, but to *keep* them out or in.

The taxi moved into gear. Jane swung around to see it pushing away from the curbside, to see Audrey closing her bag, tossing her head to one side, stepping forwards towards the first of the four stone steps.

"Don't tell me you haven't *rung* yet."

"I don't know," said Jane. "I mean, I don't know, which one?"

"The one with my damned name on it, of course."

"Sorry, I . . . Augy?"

They were both on the top step by now. Behind them, the street was silent.

"Augy, it's been a pretty good day, hasn't it?"

Audrey hit the bell beside the card marked "Croft, Flat J."

A car, its tires screaming, twisted itself into the side street.

Jane said, "I've had a fantastic time. Hey, was I disgusting when I was pissed? *You* were. You were awful."

"Oh, for goodness' . . . Come on, woman. *Answer*, then."

"Maybe she isn't in or something."

The car that had entered the street roared towards them, its headlights exploding the dusk, its engine yelling.

Audrey slammed the bell push again with the heel of her hand and leaned her weight against it, as, behind them, brakes bit, rubber strained against metal, engine roar rose to a hard, tight crescendo and, immediately, died.

In the new soundlessness, a car door squeaked open.

Both girls turned.

Stepping around the hood of a long, low, soft-topped sports car was a man, the fingers of his left hand gripped about the necks of two wine bottles.

"Good evening, ladies. Might I be of any help to either one of you?" he asked.

Part 3

10

"Oh, hello, Gary," said Audrey.

"My, what an affectionate greeting!" The man was still smiling, was still walking towards them. The bottles dangling from the grip of his curled fingers banged against one another as he moved.

"It brings tears to my eyes to see how deeply you've been missing me," he said, as he reached the step beneath the one on which the girls were standing, as he stilled the clang of the bottles against his thigh.

Although his face was now on a level with theirs, he wasn't tall, for a man, and his body, close to, seemed slighter, more compact and slimmer than it had when he'd strode around the hood of his car. He wore a leather jacket undone at the front, a white, cotton shirt, faded jeans and sneakers. His brown hair was curly and short and clung to the planes of his head. He smelled of tobacco, of lemons.

"Aren't you going to kiss me, then, little Audrey?"

63

His voice had a singsong quality, a full, warm music that cradled his words.

"That's better. How are you, anyway? Have you had a good day?"

"Okay," said Audrey, shrugging, and Jane turned to look at her, astonished, disappointed that none of the tension had left her voice or her face. The man's arrival had had no effect on her. His appearance, which Jane had felt like a shock of hope, had left Audrey quite unmoved.

The hope turned stale in Jane's mouth. She looked at her shoes.

The man said, "And what about your friend? Don't you think you might introduce us?"

"Oh," said Audrey. "Plain, that's Gary Clifford, my brother-in-law."

"Yes. How do you do?" said Jane.

"Very well, thank you. And you?"

Then Audrey swung away from them both and hit the bell push once more.

"What's she *doing*, for goodness' sake?"

"Isn't she answering?" asked Gary. "Oh dear. That must mean she's too busy shouting at Henny to hear you."

"Is Henny up there?"

"Yes. Where did you think? She came around earlier to help your mum with the supper. Not, as you can imagine, that her help was required, or even *wanted*. Still, some people never learn. . . ."

As he spoke, Gary climbed to join the two girls on the top step. Then he bent his knees and lowered his mouth to a brass grille, which Jane hadn't previously noticed, at the bottom of the column of bell pushes.

"Come on, Lucrezia," he shouted. "We're giving you up to three. After that, you can stuff your supper and we'll go and get pissed somewhere else. Do you hear me? One! Two! Thr . . ."

Immediately, from the grille into which he was shouting, came an answering voice: a machine-gun explosion of dislocated vowel sounds, followed by a dull, mechanical hum. Jane gasped. Gary pushed at the center of the double doors, swinging them open and inwards.

"See you both up there," said Audrey, sprinting past them, running away from them, disappearing around the angle of an ill-lit, carpeted stairway.

Jane lurched to follow her; then stopped, disorientated. The fraying line by which she'd been tied to Audrey all day seemed suddenly to have snapped, to have broken completely.

She felt a hard lump begin to form in her throat; then swallowed it, because she wasn't alone. Gary, Audrey's brother-in-law, was standing in the entrance hall beside her. She must say something.

"I've never seen one of those before."

"What," said Gary, "the intercom?"

"Yes."

Jane looked at him. His eyes, green, with brown flecks and a ring of dark brown around each iris, were still smiling.

She said, "I . . . It gave me quite a fright."

"She couldn't hear what I was saying, you know. Audrey's mum."

"Oh, couldn't she?"

"No. Or isn't that what you're looking so worried about?"

"What? Oh, am I? Sorry. I didn't . . ."

"There's no need to be sorry."

Gary lifted the bottles he was carrying and tucked them between his body and his left arm, as though he were about to do something, as though he were about to touch her. Then, instead, he laughed and said, "Come on, I think we'd better go *up* there. We'll take the lift, shall we? This way."

He strode away from her along the hall and pulled back the gates to a lift.

"After you . . . What's your *real* name?" he asked.

"Jane. Jane Rackham."

"Is that why they call you Plain, then? Because it rhymes?"

"Yes. Well, you know. Plain Jane. It's a nickname. Like Augy, or . . ."

"I still don't think it's terribly appropriate. If you don't mind, I shall refrain from using it. After you, Miss Rackham."

Still holding the gates, he extended his right arm and guided her into the lift.

The gates closed. The gates clanged shut. The dim, narrow cabin became filled with the incense of leather, tobacco and lemons.

A button was pressed. The cabin juddered, then rose on whining wires.

"Have you met them yet, or is this the first time?"

"Sorry, what?" said Jane.

"Audrey's family. Henny and Lucrezia."

"Lu . . . ?"

"Mrs. Croft. Mum."

"Oh, yes, I met her this morning. She came to the station. I didn't . . . I didn't know that was her name."

Gary laughed.

"It isn't. But don't tell me they haven't taught you about the Borgias yet, in that expensive school of yours."

"Oh, I see."

"What did you think of her?"

"What?" said Jane.

"Sorry. You're quite right. I shouldn't have asked that. All right, Miss Rackham, out you get. We're here."

The lift gates opened again, onto a corridor more narrow than the entrance hall, but equally dim and carpeted. At one end, away to the right, a door stood ajar, thrusting into the passageway a wedge of light and the sounds of incoherent voices.

"On you go, then. Don't worry, I'm right behind you."

There being no alternative, Jane began to walk forwards. Gary at her back, she passed through the half-open doorway. She crossed a small, square vestibule.

She entered into Mrs. Croft's kitchen.

"Jane! Hello, dear! We were beginning . . . Good evening, Gareth."

"Evening, Mrs. C."

"Hello, Mrs. Croft."

"Plain!" said Audrey, swinging around from her seat on a white, Formica-topped table. "Where on earth have you two been?"

Jane said, "We came up in the lift."

"Lazy cows! Hey, Plain, this is my sister, Henny."

67

"How do you do?"

"How do you do, Plain? Gary, darling, did you remember the wine?"

"Of course. Here! Catch!"

"Don't be stupid."

"Gareth, will you kindly behave yourself?"

"Oh, Mummy, he wasn't really going to chuck them. He wouldn't dare."

"And you, Audrey darling, haven't I asked you *twice* to get *down* from there? I don't mean to . . ."

"Okay!"

The brightly lit room exploded about Jane's head with its movement and noise. Gary, having removed his leather jacket, flourished it, then draped it across the back of a steel-framed chair. Audrey jumped down from the table. Mrs. Croft, an apron protecting her lace-trimmed blouse and her long, velvet skirt, brandished a spoon and screamed at Gary to hang his jacket somewhere else. Henrietta, tall and slim like her mother with long, dark hair and the enormous, brown Croft eyes, chopped parsley, holding the knife at either end, like a chef.

Jane gripped her bag in both hands.

It was going to be all right.

She'd been mad, she'd been *stupid* to think that it wouldn't. What *had* she imagined?

From the oven came a rich, warm smell of garlic and wine and meat. On the top of the cooker, vegetables danced in their pans of boiling water. The window above the sink was curtained with steam. Audrey was saying, "For goodness' sake, Plain, take your coat off. You are supposed to be *staying*, you know."

"Yes. Sorry. I . . ."

"Why don't you show Jane to her room, baby? And the bathroom. I expect she'd like to tidy up. Wouldn't you, darling?"

"Yes, thank you, Mrs. Croft."

"Okay, Plain, this way. Follow me. Hey, Henny, don't do the pudding till I come back. I want to help you. Come *on*, Plain."

It was going to be all right.

Whatever it was that Jane had imagined, that morning, in the station, whatever it was that she'd thought she'd glimpsed in Audrey's face then, or heard in Mrs. Croft's voice, whatever dread she'd felt later, on leaving the cinema, on climbing down from the taxi, on entering, with Gary, through the half-open doorway of the flat, was buried, now, beneath the storm of motion and sound, was lost in the confusion of voices, the clatter of dishes, the familiar hurry to brush her hair and tidy her face and wash her hands before dinner.

II

Her plate piled high with scoops of chocolate mousse, a glass of wine at her elbow, a cream jug being passed to her by Henrietta, and Audrey saying, "Plain's okay, and a couple of others, but you should see *most* of them. Gross, pimply morons, most of them, aren't they, Plain?" Jane's conviction that the weekend was going to be fine grew stronger and ever more confident. The hints and whispers that something was wrong, that something ugly was poised to spring, had become unbelievable, improbable, an old, ridiculous dream.

Her face was warm and heavy, but she wasn't drunk. Her fingers still had their power of feeling as they closed around the silver stomach of the cream jug, as they tilted this to the exact angle at which the cream, thick in the furrow of the jug's lip, overflowed and dropped onto the dark and granular mousse. A warm, easy sigh escaped her. She handed the jug to Gary, who was sitting on her right.

On *his* right, at the head of the dining table, was Mrs. Croft. On her right, Audrey; on Audrey's, Henrietta. The bottom of the table was occupied by an empty bread basket, a bowl of apples, bananas and grapes, a tray of cheeses and plates stacked up from three previous courses.

Across the windows at the far end of the room, curtains were drawn. Soft light spilled over the rim of shell-shaped lampshades set high around the walls.

Audrey said, "What about Ruth Bottomly? Do you think Gary'd like *her*?"

Jane laughed.

Running his index finger around the lip of the cream jug, Gary said, "With a name like that, who could fail to?"

Jane said, "It's not just her name, Gary. She's *enormous*. She weighs about hundred and fifty pounds. Really. And she's got this great, fat face, with black eyebrows and a black mustache, like those old pictures of John Bull, you know. And she snores. Goodness she snores."

"I'd be disappointed to hear that she didn't," said Gary.

Audrey said, "She's in Plain's dormitory."

"Worse luck," said Jane. "You've got a *much* better lot of people. Nicky Lawrence and Randy Spurling and Prevy . . ."

"Nicky's okay," said Audrey.

Then Mrs. Croft said, "But darling, I thought you and Jane were in the *same* dormitory. Aren't you? I was under the impression you were inseparable. I thought you couldn't *live* without one another. You should have seen them this morning, Gareth, a⊚ the station. Darling Jane, wide-eyed and openmouthed, obviously terrified to take a step, or make *any* decision whatsoever, without Audrey's say-so . . ."

There was a moment's stillness, a moment in which nothing happened. Jane's breath stuck thick in her throat.

"Oh, for goodness' sake, Mummy," said Audrey, "don't be so ridiculous. Just because we didn't want to have lunch at . . ."

"Nonsense! It was touching. I do wish you'd seen them, Gareth."

Jane stared through the spoonful of mousse that was poised halfway between her plate and her open mouth.

But, before the sudden tension in the dining room had had time to stretch any further, to crack apart, Henrietta shook a king-sized cigarette from the packet on the table beside her, flung out her hand to Gary for his lighter and said, "Anyway, what about the staff, Augy? Do you still have Old Bailey for math? As far as I can remember, she spent more time reading lurid crime novels than actually *teaching*. You wouldn't believe it, Gary, the standard of education in that place."

She laughed, her voice as sharp and clear as glass splinters. She lit her cigarette. She handed the lighter back to Gary.

She said, "And I suppose the Termite's still got all those cats. Has she, Augy? If you had to go into her study for something, you couldn't sit down for cats. They were everywhere, as though they owned the place. Oh, and I remember there was one particularly nasty tabby, gigantic, the size of a puma, I'm not exaggerating, who used to terrorize the whole school. He used to get into the kitchen, sometimes, and if one of the maids tried to shoo him away he'd blow himself up to even bigger than he normally was and spit at them. You could hear them screaming from the Assembly Hall. Unbelievable."

She blew a long column of smoke towards the ceiling.

Jane looked around. The silence, again, was anybody's. Audrey was watching her sister with pleasure and with admiration, but with no intention, it seemed, of answering her original question. Gary was weaving his cigarette lighter backwards and forwards, backwards and forwards through hard, square fingers. Mrs. Croft stared straight ahead, down the table's length, her brown eyes tight, a meaningless smile on her mouth.

Jane filled her lungs. She licked her lips.

"Pythagoras," she said. "That's the name of the tabby. Only he's quite old, now. It's the kitten, Aziz, the new kitten, who gets into all the trouble. D'you remember, Augy, when he climbed in through the chapel window and got onto the altar and knocked over all the communion wine? We all thought the vicar was going to have to lick it up himself. You know, what with it being consecrated. Anyway, he didn't, but it was jolly funny. You should have

72

seen the Termite's face, not knowing whether to cuddle him, or beat him. Aziz, I mean. Not the vicar. D'you remember, Augy?"

"Yes," said Audrey, her eyes reluctantly turning from Henrietta's face to Jane's.

"Do you?"

"Yes, of course."

She shrugged. She stretched for her glass of wine.

She said, "The whole thing's pathetic, if you ask me."

"What?" asked Gary.

The room was beginning to relax again, to breathe again, to live.

"*What*'s pathetic, O sister-in-law?"

"The Termite and her cats. As far as *she*'s concerned, they're like her *children* or something. I mean, you'd think ninety of *us* would be enough to satisfy her frustrated maternal whatsit, wouldn't you? Without having to resort to animals."

"Given the choice between cats and schoolgirls," said Gary, "I can assure you that I'd have *no* hesitation in choosing the former."

Everyone laughed, except for Mrs. Croft.

Gary turned to her.

"Will it bother you if I smoke now, Mother dear?" he asked.

"Please don't call me that, Gareth. And you can see very well that Henrietta's already smoking."

Mrs. Croft's voice was strained. Snapping her lips shut, she lowered her fork and spoon to her plate and clicked their handles together. She lifted a strand of gray hair from her forehead and trailed it backwards over the top of her head.

73

But Gary appeared to notice none of this, as he smiled, as he narrowed his eyes to inhale on a black cheroot. And Henrietta had begun to talk about the school once more, was remembering an old German mistress who'd insisted on spreading everything she ate, even pudding, with mustard, and Audrey was interrupting her, was saying, "What about the Haggis, Plain? You know how she puts salt in her *coffee*. Go on, show Henrietta. Show her how she does it. Plain's really good at this, Henny."

"For goodness' sake, Aug."

"No, please, I'd love to see it," said Henrietta.

"Oh, okay."

Jane pursed her lips. She held her breath to turn her face red, raised one hand several inches above the table, crooked its little finger and then, her features pinched into an expression of refined concentration, rubbed together the index finger and thumb.

"It accentuates the wee *flavor*, girls," she said. "You should try it on your porrage, you really should. Oh, yes, *and* on chocolate ice cream. A wee dram of salt does *wonders* for the flavor of chocolate."

Everyone laughed: Henrietta with the clear, splintered sound she'd made before, her head tilted back, the tips of her long, slim fingers propping the point of her chin; Gary with a deeper, lazier sound, his eyelids heavy; Audrey with relief and pride in her friend's success, and in her own, for having engineered it; Jane with happiness. The evening was turning out just as she'd imagined, just as she'd hoped when Audrey had first invited her.

Or *almost* was. *Would* have been had a slice of the laughter surrounding the table not stayed frozen by Mrs. Croft's silence, her tight-lipped withdrawal, her glazed, hard eyes.

Why? Why, every time that Jane thought that the evening was saved, did some shiver of tension, like this, slip in to imperil it? Her imitation of the Haggis hadn't been *that* funny, she knew, but it wasn't only through lack of amusement that Mrs. Croft wasn't laughing. There was something else, some unresolved emotion that lurked beneath the surface of whatever else appeared to be taking place in the room.

At that moment, Mrs. Croft rose from her seat to clear the table. Jane rose, too, with an offer of help. But at once Mrs. Croft said, "No, dear, *leave* it all, *please.* Why don't you just carry on with your funny little story?"

And the sarcasm hummed through the room, even after Mrs. Croft had left it.

"Well," said Gary, at last, "I'm sorry that you don't like your teachers. But I daresay that *they* don't think much of *you*, either."

As though emerging from a short trance, Audrey said, "What? Oh, the staff love us. Well, they love me. Doesn't the Termite think I'm a lovely, thoughtful person, Plain?"

"That's only because you suck up to her," said Jane, forcing herself to concentrate, to forget the woman who'd just left. "You should hear her, Gary, Henny. All '*Thank* you, Miss Anthony. How *super*, Miss Anthony.' No wonder she likes you. It's nauseating."

"Well? It works, doesn't it?"

"You're a whore."

"Who's talking, old Plain Face Rackham? Who was making eyes at strange men on the bus this morning?"

"Not *me*. Oh, that man with the acne! Not *me*. And it

75

certainly wasn't me who flirted with that barman in the pub. Hunching your shoulders in to make your tits look bigger! He was almost climbing over the counter to get at you. The only person you didn't flirt with, all day, was the man in the jewelers and only 'cause he was queer."

"Yes, wasn't he? You should've seen him, Henny."

"Is that the jewelers where you got the bracelet?" asked Henrietta.

"What bracelet's this?" asked Gary. "Let's see."

Audrey shook her wrist and the sliver of silver links escaped from the cuff of her sleeve, to hang, burning amber, around the width of her hand.

"Only this," she said.

"It's very nice," said Gary.

"Yes, isn't it?" said Henrietta. "The girls bought it this afternoon, apparently. Augy showed it to me earlier."

"It's more than *nice*, though," said Jane. "It's beautiful. Look, Gary, it's so perfectly made. It's fantastic. Honestly, it's the most wonderful bit of jewelry I've ever seen."

She looked at Audrey, who was drawing her hand back over the tabletop. Audrey glanced at Jane, then tossed her head and swung her gaze to the far side of the room, disassociating herself from the naive enthusiasm. But she couldn't help smiling, after all, couldn't help turning her eyes back to Jane's and smiling with her.

"It really is beautiful," said Jane, to Audrey alone this time.

And Audrey's smile spread, defeating the expression of carelessness that she was trying to impose on her lips. Her eyes locked with Jane's, recreating, for a moment, the day that they'd spent together: the glasses of gin that they'd drunk, under age, in a pub; the drowsy warmth of the afternoon in the park; the X-rated film that they'd seen together. . . .

"*Aud*rey?"

The current broke.

"*Ba*by?"

The current snapped, lashing backwards to slice across Jane's smile.

"Let me see, darling. What's this lovely thing you're showing everybody?"

Jane's cheeks burned. Her hands felt for something, anything, the edge of the table and a pepper mill, to play with.

"Come on, baby."

"It isn't *anything*, Mummy."

"Don't tell me it's a secret. I could hear dear Jane enthusing from the kitchen. You've got a very strong voice, darling. Let me see, baby. Show me what this 'beautiful' thing is. It can't be such a *terrible* secret if you've already shown Henrietta."

"It's only a bracelet, for God's sake."

Jane tipped the pepper grinder from side to side, trailing a line of brown dust over the tablecloth.

Henrietta rested her head on one hand.

Mrs. Croft said, "Well, what *is* this? Is everybody allowed to see except me?"

"For goodness' sake, it's not *that* damn wonderful," said Audrey, wrenching her sleeve back, thrusting her arm towards her mother.

"Oh," said Mrs. Croft. "Oh, I see. It's *that* bracelet, is it? I suppose Jane encouraged you to go and waste your money on that. You do know it's probably not even sterling silver? There isn't a hallmark on it, is there? Or didn't you look to see? Did you? Jane, did *you* look to see if the bracelet was hallmarked?"

"I . . . I'm sorry, I don't know what . . ."

"You don't know what a *hall*mark is, darling? I thought you knew everything about jewelry, from the way you were going on just now. Oh well, the damage is done, I suppose. . . ."

"Lucrezia! Please! Your daughter hasn't been *raped*."

At the sound of Gary's deep, laughing voice, the air seeped back into Jane's lungs, the pulse resumed its beating in her forehead. She let go of the pepper grinder. She pushed some hair from her face.

"Those terrible, tragic tones! You sound as though she'd been done out of her virginity, not a few pounds. Besides, it is silver. I've seen it myself."

"Thank you, Gareth, but I think we can do without your opinion. You don't know what this whole thing . . ."

"Oh, come on, Mummy," said Henrietta. "Gary is right. You're making an awful lot of fuss about nothing."

"And thank you too, darling. How nice to see you taking your husband's side. It makes a change from seeing you all tight-lipped and martyred because he hasn't been home for two nights running, because he's been out on the tiles somewhere, spending your hard-earned money."

"I think, *this* time, it's your opinion we can do without, Mrs. C."

"Oh, Gareth, don't think it matters to me. If Henrietta chooses to keep you until you finish writing your great theatrical masterpiece—or *start* it, more accurately—why should *I* care? If she chooses to put up with your drinking and your . . . Well, anyway, that's entirely her business. She probably enjoys it. Don't you, darling? You rather like suffering, in a quiet, nondescript sort of way."

"And my *what?*" asked Gary. "Put up with my drinking and my *what*, were you going to say?"

"Look, please . . ." said Henrietta.

Jane stared at Audrey, trying to find her eyes again, trying to regain the contact that they'd had a few minutes before. But Audrey was watching her mother, was watching her with a white and frightening intensity.

"Augy?" said Jane.

But she might as well not have bothered.

"You know very well *what*, Gareth," said Mrs. Croft. "But I really don't think this is *quite* the moment. . . ."

"Well I just wish you'd thought of that sooner," said Henrietta.

"Oh, dear, is the worm turning?"

"Augy, please!" said Jane. "Augy, please, let's go to your room or something."

But Audrey was pushing herself to her feet, was lunging across the table towards her mother, was opening her mouth, was screaming, "Shut up! Just shut up, damn you! Why do you always have to get at *Henny*? Do you think I like that, or something? Don't you know it makes me sick?"

"Darling! Baby! Remember yourself!"

"I *am* remembering. Always! Always it's *her* who . . ."

"Augy," said Jane, standing up also, reaching across the rumpled cloth, the empty glasses, the disordered place mats to grab her friend's arm.

"And *you* can go to hell too. Just keep out of this. You don't know the first thing about it. Go away. Haven't you made enough trouble for one evening?"

"Yes, Jane, please, would you *mind* your own business?" said Mrs. Croft.

Jane's eyes stung. Her face flared red again and her stunned breath threatened to choke her. That the ingredients of this scene had been lying around the flat all evening made it no less shocking now that, at last, they'd come together. Mother and daughters, sisters and mother, shouting at each other, swearing at each other, hating each other so much that their faces had become deformed and their voices ugly.

"Why on *earth* couldn't you have had the decency to wait till we were alone for this?" Henrietta was asking, her fingers tangled in her long, thick hair, her brown eyes shining.

"For *what?*" asked Mrs. Croft. "It's not *me* who's making a scene. Besides, I hardly ever get to see Audrey alone or otherwise. She couldn't even bear to have lunch with me today. . . ."

"Do you bloody well *blame* me?" asked Audrey. White spit flew to her chin.

"Augy, all right, please," said Henrietta. "You know she didn't mean that, Mummy."

"Yes I did. Don't *crawl* to her, Henny."

"Baby! What *is* this? What's got *in*to you?"

Abruptly, Gary pushed back his chair and crushed his cheroot in an ashtray. Now, everybody but Henrietta was standing, while around them their chairs lurched higgledy-piggledy, like drunks thrown out of a pub. Linen napkins lay crumpled on the carpet. A boiling kettle, from the kitchen, screamed.

Gary took Jane's wrist in his left hand.

"Come on, Miss Rackham, let's go and make some coffee, shall we?" he said.

12

They were in the kitchen. Gary closed the door behind them. Then he walked across to the serving hatch that opened into the dining room and closed that.

He unplugged the electric kettle. It continued to whistle for several seconds after he had done so, filling the room with its noise and with its steam.

When the whistle had died, he pointed to a shelf above Jane's head and said, "The beans are up there."

They could still hear the voices next door. They were muffled now, it was true, and incoherent, but each in turn identified its owner. Audrey's was loud and metallic, Henrietta's plaintive, while Mrs. Croft's soared, hovered, then plummeted, like a bird of prey on the wing.

Some words broke loose from the general rumble: "Baby!" "Mummy!" "For goodness' *sake!*"

Jane stared at the serving hatch as though mesmerized, not by *it*, but by what was taking place beyond it. Her every sense was focused on that oblong of white Formica with its inset, chrome handle, its smudges of fingerprints, its trickles of dried tomato sauce, or gravy, or red wine.

"I said the coffee beans are just above your head."

"Yes," said Jane.

"Then I wonder if you'd mind passing them to me. Miss Rackham? Look, ignore them, girl. They might go on like that for hours."

Jane withdrew her eyes from the hatch. Not focusing on anything else, however, she reached up and tapped along the row of glass jars that stood on the shelf above her.

"The one marked Coffee," said Gary.

"Yes," said Jane.

She gripped a jar, lifted it from the shelf, lowered it to her chest and held it there.

"That one says Rice—Brown," said Gary.

Then Jane began to cry.

"I'm sorry," she said. "I'm sorry, Gary. I . . . I'm sorry. I . . ."

"Good heavens."

"I'm sorry."

She tilted her face to the ceiling, gasping for air. She rocked the jar of brown rice against her body. The tears slid down the sides of her face and into her ears and down her neck, dampening the collar of her blouse.

She curled herself around the jar and clenched her eyes shut.

"I'm sorry," she said. "I don't know . . . I'm sorry."

"Okay, okay. Okay. Shhh! Here. Here. Shhh!"

She felt Gary squeeze himself in front of her, between where she stood and the kitchen wall.

"Come on, what is it?"

He eased the jar from her hands and put it somewhere else. He took her hands in his and began to rub them. The rest of her body, her head, her neck, her torso, her legs, were rigid and arched like a bow away from him, preventing him from getting any closer.

She hadn't meant to cry. For once, she hadn't even been worried that she might be about to. There'd been no warning, none of the usual signs that told her she was in danger of making a fool of herself, that allowed her to clamp the necessary restraints upon her voice and her face.

"What is it, Jane?"

"Nothing. I don't know. I . . ."

She was helpless. She didn't even know *why* she was crying, not *now*, not when she'd managed to prevent herself from doing so all day, all week, ever since the letter from her father . . .

No! What had *that* got to do with anything?

"Nothing! I don't know," she said, opening her eyes and lifting her face to look at a blurred Gary, who, one eyebrow raised higher than the other, his bottom lip pushed up to cover his top one, was frowning down at her.

As soon as he saw that she was watching him, he changed his expression. It became a smile.

"That's stupid, isn't it?" he asked. "Crying about nothing? People've been put into straightjackets for less than that. And all that mascara running down your face! You look like a chimney sweep. Here."

With his right hand, he drew a handkerchief from the back pocket of his jeans. He squeezed it into a ball and dabbed Jane's face with it.

She twisted away from him, but his left hand held her.

"Come back," he said. "All right, all right, finish the crying then. You might as well, now you've started."

And, while Jane was still catching for air to speak, he

pulled her towards him again and cupped her head against his shoulder.

"Cry it all out of you, then," he said, his body rocking, the palm of his hand stroking Jane's hair. "That's right. Let it go. Nobody's going to hear you. They're all far too busy next door. Is that what upset you, then? That little display of family affection back there? You shouldn't have let it, you know. They really can't help themselves."

He laid his face against the crown of Jane's head, so that he was talking into her hair.

"You know, I lied to you before," he said. "They're not *really* the Borgias. Not even Italian at all. No, what they *actually* are is Rumanian. Very old family, in fact. Aristocrats. You've probably heard of them. The Draculas! That was Lucrezia's maiden name, Dracula. They won't admit to it, of course, none of them. But you'll notice, when you get to know them better, that at the end of every meal, no matter how much they've eaten, how much *boeuf Bourguignon* and chocolate mousse they've stuffed themselves with, they *have* to finish up with a drop of blood. They'd *die* without it. It's a fact."

By now, Jane was laughing. She was still crying, but was laughing, too, her breath escaping in short, staccato bursts that were immediately trapped in the warmth of Gary's shirt.

Gary said, "You know why Mrs. C. eats all that delicatessen muck, all those pâtés and smoked sausages and so on? She's trying to build up a resistance to garlic. And I daresay you've noticed those funny faces they all pull from time to time, when they think no one's looking. Yes! *You* know. Clamping their lips together, like this . . ."

He lifted his face from Jane's head and stood back from her, so that she could see him. He'd squeezed his mouth shut over cheeks swollen with air.

Releasing the air, he said, "It's their teeth. It's so that you won't notice their teeth have suddenly grown enormous. They all do it. I mean, Henrietta! I *never* let Henny kiss me after the sun's gone down. I did, once, and I've still got the scars to show for it."

Letting go of Jane's hands, he pulled the collar of his shirt away from his neck and twisted his head to one side.

"Well, this light isn't very good," he said, "but I'll show you tomorrow, in the daylight."

Through her sobs and her laughter, Jane sniffed. She exhaled and the breath flowed from her in an almost steady stream. She sniffed again, less loudly this time.

"Okay," she said.

Gary gave her his handkerchief.

"Thanks," she said, stepping back from him, testing the steadiness of her legs, her hands, her rib cage.

"But I still don't . . . I mean, was it something to do with *me*, or something?"

"You?" said Gary. "Good heavens, no. I told you, they're like that every time they get together. Oh, sweetheart, Lucrezia's got nothing against *you*, personally. You mustn't think that for a moment. It's just that you're Audrey's friend, don't you see? And by undermining *you*, she's undermining *Audrey*. It's as simple as that."

He smiled again, his green eyes puckered, his mouth twisted down at either corner.

Jane looked away from him. She picked up the jar of brown rice that he'd placed on the kitchen table. She tilted

85

it. The grains whispered among each other, then settled into a new position on their curved glass bed.

When the row had exploded, in all its ugliness, over the dining-room table, she'd thought that the danger that she'd sensed all day had been met. But it hadn't, not entirely. She saw that now. For behind the row was the *reason* for the row and, if that wasn't her, which she'd never really supposed, then what *was* it? It wasn't enough to be told that they always behaved like that. *Why* did they? Jane had to know.

And Gary, she felt certain, could tell her, could help her to understand. Unlike Audrey, he wasn't too much involved. Even though married to Henrietta, there was something about him, some clear, almost cruel detachment, some detached strength which Jane felt sure she could trust. If only . . . No, she should be *pleased* that he didn't condescend to her, that he made jokes about the Crofts with her, that he treated her, sometimes, as though she were an adult like himself. Besides, who else was there to turn to but him?

She rolled the jar of brown rice between her hands.

"But why should she *want* to?" she asked.

"Why should *who* want to do *what*?"

"Mrs. Croft. Why should she want to undermine Audrey?"

"Oh! Why, to make Audrey love her, of course. Yes, I know, it doesn't make a *lot* of sense, but Lucrezia's remarkably irrational at times, as I daresay you've noticed."

"But . . ."

"Look, all *she* can see is that Audrey's growing up, growing away from her, so she does what she can to make her a baby again. A baby who loves her. Do you see?"

"No!" said Jane. "I mean, why does she think . . . ? Of *course* Augy loves her."

"Well, you may be right. I don't . . ."

"Of *course* she does. She's her mother, for goodness' sake."

"Oh, I see. Well now, *that* doesn't prove anything, you know."

"Yes it does. It's . . . I mean . . . Well, families just *do* love each other. Parents and children, they love each other. It's . . . It's . . ."

"What?" asked Gary.

"Well, they just *do*. That's all."

"Do they?"

He was watching her, no longer smiling, his green eyes grown narrow and thoughtful. With one hand, he reached up to take the jar of coffee beans from its shelf. Then he walked away from her to a work surface where an electric grinder stood, and poured some beans into the grinder's cup.

For a moment, Jane was alarmed, thinking that she'd driven him away, but before she could apologize, he said, "You're a complicated child, aren't you? Asking so many questions, then refusing to listen to the answers. What am I supposed to do with you?"

"I don't know," said Jane, too relieved that he was still talking to her to listen properly to what he said. "I'm sorry, really. I didn't mean to be rude. Please go on."

"Are you sure you want me to?"

"Yes. Of course."

"Okay. Well, for a start, you do know that Mrs. Croft's divorced, don't you?"

"Yes. Yes, I did . . ."

"Well, that's not really the important thing, but a divorce can highlight lots of things that mightn't otherwise have been so obvious. For example, in this case, Henny used to be very much her dad's little girl. So what's wrong with that, you might ask, and you'd be right. Until, that is, Dad runs away from home and Mum starts hating Dad and *you* go on *loving* Dad, until Mum starts hating *you.* Do you see what I mean? In other words, while Lucrezia may never have been particularly fond of Henny in the first place, she now positively dislikes her. And Audrey, who was always her favorite anyway, she worships. My baby! You've heard her. My little baby! The only person I've got left in the world! Well, that *is* how Lucrezia sees it. And, because she does, she clings. And, because she clings, Audrey struggles. It's almost inevitable. While poor, dear, sweet old Henny, of course, would do anything in her power for one *smile,* one *word* of *approval* from her mum. It's sad, I admit, but quite understandable. Don't you think?"

Gary looked at Jane, the thumb of his right hand poised against the starter button of the coffee grinder. Then, when she didn't answer, he depressed the button, so that the blades burst into crackling action against the beans.

For a minute, the kitchen was filled with their noise.

When it was over, when Gary'd released the button, unscrewed the grinder's lid and begun to tip the soft, brown powder into a paper filter, Jane said, "I see. I didn't know. Augy . . . I mean, Augy never talks about that. About her papa and the divorce and so on. . . ."

"But that's not what *I* was talking about, either. I said

88

at the beginning, Miss Rackham, that the divorce just high-lighted things that were already there. What I was *trying* to explain was that it's naive to assume that parents and children automatically love each other, *like* each other, are *kind* to each other, even. Loving and kindness just aren't automatic things. They have to be worked at, thought about. Oh, oh, when you're a *baby*, of course, there's no question about it. At least, in some cases, even then . . . But no, usually, it's when you begin to grow up, like Audrey and you are doing, when you begin to become a person in your own right, *that*'s when the conflict starts. Come on, you must know what I'm talking about. Haven't there been moments, with your own parents . . . ?"

"No!" said Jane.

"Hang on! I haven't even finished what I was going to say yet."

"Well, there haven't. I know what you were going to say. You mustn't assume that all families are like . . ."

"The Crofts?"

Suddenly, Gary laughed.

Still laughing, he shook the coffee grounds to the bottom of the paper filter, placed the paper filter inside a plastic filter and stood the lot on the neck of a tall, brown jug. Then he reached for the electric kettle and poured water, still steaming, over the grounds.

"No," he said at last, "I assure you, I don't assume *that* for one moment. If all families were like them . . . !"

He glanced at the serving hatch, from behind which a murmur of voices still rose and fell, but with less energy now. It was no longer easy to tell who was speaking, or if more than one person was.

"Believe me, I didn't mean *that*. But all the same, don't tell me there aren't *moments* when you feel . . . well, that your parents don't understand you, or that *you* don't understand *them*, or . . ."

"No," said Jane, "there aren't. It's not like that."

"Okay," said Gary, looking up at her again, the smile becoming more gentle upon his lips and around his eyes. "Okay. It doesn't matter. I don't believe you, but it doesn't matter. If you don't want to admit it yet . . . But I've a feeling you're about to, all the same, that and a lot of other things. Oh, come on, there's no need to scowl at me. You've no idea how ferocious you look, with those knotted brows and those deep, gray eyes like thunderstorms. Come on, give me a smile, Miss Rackham."

Relieved at the change in the subject of conversation, Jane smiled.

"Anyway," she said, "my eyes aren't gray."

"More gray than blue. And very lovely, when you're not frowning."

"What? My eyes? With that horrid scar over one of them?"

"It's an enchanting scar. It's an enchanting face, come to that."

"Don't be stupid," said Jane, aware that he was humoring her now, aware that a distance had come between them, but glad, in a way, for the space.

The row next door must surely be over by now. Surely Audrey would come in soon, to find out where she had got to.

"Yes, that *was* stupid," said Gary. "If you knew you were beautiful, you'd certainly become less so. Right! We'll change the subject, shall we? Tomorrow! What are your plans for tomorrow?"

"Oh, I don't know," said Jane.

"Haven't you decided yet?"

"Well, I don't know. Maybe Augy has."

"Then we must ask her. But if you *haven't* got anything planned, what would you say to us all driving down to the river? For a picnic, maybe. As long as the weather's all right."

"Yes. Fine. Yes, that sounds fantastic."

"Good. And, Miss Rackham? You're okay now, are you?"

"What?" asked Jane. "Oh, that! Yes. I'm sorry. I don't know what . . . Just . . . I mean, I'm probably just tired or something. That's all."

"Yes," said Gary. "Yes, I expect that's all. But look, sweetheart, if ever . . ."

Then, by an amount that could not have been measured it was so small, his expression changed and he was no longer looking at her, but at somebody standing in the doorway behind her.

"It's time we were going, Gary. Hello, Jane, I'm really sorry about . . . *You* know. Anyway, I'm sure Gary's been looking after you. Darling? Come on. Where's your jacket?"

Henrietta already had her coat on. Her mouth was smiling, but her eyes were tired.

She said, "Well, good-bye, Jane. I'm glad we met. Perhaps we'll see you again sometime."

"Tomorrow," said Gary, still at his place by the work surface, and, without knowing why, Jane wished that he

91

hadn't said it. She would have liked to have gone to find Audrey, but Henrietta blocked the kitchen doorway.

"We'll be seeing the girls again tomorrow," said Gary, reaching to lift his jacket from the back of a steel-framed chair.

"What are you talking about, darling? Of course we won't. I'm working tomorrow. It's my Sunday at the studio. You know that."

"So it is. I'd forgotten. Still, that doesn't stop *me*, does it?"

"I thought you'd got some writing you wanted to do."

"It'll keep. The girls' weekend out's more important. I thought I'd take them down to the river. You don't mind, do you?"

"No. You know very well I don't. But don't you think you ought to ask Mummy first?"

"Most certainly. But I hardly think she's likely to want to come too."

"You *know* that's not what I mean," said Henrietta. "She hasn't seen an *awful* lot of Augy this weekend. Look, look, why don't you leave it that you'll ring and see how things are in the morning? All right, darling? Now, please, shall we go? Jane, Augy's along in the drawing room."

"Thanks," said Jane.

But Gary said, "What about the coffee?"

"I'm sure Jane won't mind taking it along," said Henrietta. "Will you? Do you mind?"

"No, of course not."

"Well then," said Gary, "until tomorrow, Miss Rackham. Sleep well."

Then he was gone.

Then Henrietta and he were gone.

Jane heard the door of the flat snap shut behind them, heard, moments later, the distant purr of the lift, the slide and clang of the lift gates, the purr again, then silence.

Suddenly, she was frightened by how empty and cold the flat seemed. She'd expected to hear Audrey's voice, calling, "Plain! For goodness' sake! What on earth are you up to?" But nothing had come.

Hearing the beat of her heart in her throat, she walked across to the work surface. Reaching it, she stopped. She raised her hands and placed them one on either side of the coffeepot. She closed her fingers and thumbs around the coffeepot, around the warmth of it, around the hard, solid strength of it.

13

"Augy?"

It was much later that night. It might even have been the early hours of the following morning; although, not having a watch, Jane couldn't be sure.

After Gary and Henrietta had left, she'd taken the coffee, with cups, saucers, spoons, sugar and milk, along to Mrs. Croft and Audrey, where the three of them had drunk in the same cold silence that had filled the flat since Gary and Henrietta had left.

Audrey had been sprawled on a sofa, her hips on the edge

of its seat, her legs stretched straight in front of her. One by one, she'd lifted some glossy fashion magazines from a pile on the table beside her, flipped through them, then dropped them to the floor.

Mrs. Croft had been sitting in a winged armchair to one side of an empty fireplace. She'd watched Jane enter with the laden tray, had made a noise, more of recognition than of thanks, had refused milk and sugar, had taken a sip from her cup and, thereafter, had sat motionless and unspeaking, her large, hooded eyes staring ahead of her at nothing.

Jane had sat beside Audrey on the sofa.

About half an hour later, Mrs. Croft had said, "I'm going to bed. You'll turn the lights out after you, won't you, baby?"

"I'm going, too," had said Audrey.

Mother and daughter had stood up. Jane had stood up.

"Good night," had said Mrs. Croft and had disappeared down the long, dim corridor of the flat.

Audrey had said, "If you want to use the bathroom, you'd better go first. You're sleeping in Henny's old room. Your case is already in there."

"Yes. Thanks," had said Jane.

She'd gone to the bedroom which had once been Henrietta's but was now nobody's: a narrow, white-painted room with one sash window, a chest o' drawers, a fitted wardrobe, a single bed and a small bedside table. The drawer in the bedside table was empty and unlined. In the wardrobe, three wire hangers hung askew. The chest o' drawers was empty. It smelt of stale spices.

She'd taken her pajamas and her sponge bag from her case. She'd changed into her pajamas. She'd gone along to

94

the bathroom, used the loo, washed her hands and face, brushed her teeth.

Now, sponge bag dangling by its drawstring from the fingers of one hand, she stood in the doorway to Audrey's bedroom.

"Augy?" she said. "Augy?"

Dark, humped bedclothes changed their shape.

"What?"

"I've finished in the bathroom. Don't you want to go?"

"No."

"Augy."

"What, for goodness' sake?"

"Can I come in?"

Audrey sat up in bed. Her face floated in the shadows like a pale and insubstantial moon.

She said, "I'm trying to get to *sleep*. What's the matter with you? Don't you know what time it is?"

"I just wanted to talk, that's all."

"Well, *I* don't."

There was a silence. The white circle that was Audrey's face sank an inch or two, as though she were relaxing the support of her arms. Then it yanked itself up again.

"God, you really made a mess of things this evening, didn't you?"

"What do you mean?" asked Jane.

"What do you damn well think? Screaming your damn head off about the bracelet, that's what. I *told* you my mother didn't want me to have it. Well . . . Well, all I can say is, thanks a lot. Thanks a bloody lot, Plain. Now, just go away and let me get some sleep, will you?"

Before the last words were spoken, the face had disappeared, flung back downwards into the darkness. A halo, an echo of light glowed for a moment in the spot where it had been, then that, too, faded.

Jane said, "I'm sorry, Augy."

She changed her sponge bag to the fingers of the other hand.

She said, "But it wasn't really my fault. I mean . . . Come on, it wasn't really my fault, was it? Anyway, it's still beautiful, whatever anyone says. Isn't it?"

She listened. She entered the room. She walked to the bed and crouched beside the pillow.

"Augy, Gary says he's going to take us out for a drive in his car tomorrow. Hey! Aug!"

She shook what was probably Audrey's shoulder beneath the blankets.

She said, "That'll be fantastic, won't it? Henny's working, but Gary says he'll take us down to the river or something. Won't that be good?"

Her voice thick beneath the covers, Audrey said, "You can go. I shan't."

Jane said, "What's the matter? Don't you like Gary? Is that what it is?"

"For goodness' sake!"

"Well, I just wondered. You didn't seem very pleased when we met him, that's all. He *is* a bit . . . cynical. But he's okay, isn't he? He's jolly funny and . . ."

"Then *you* go."

"Not without you!"

"*I*'m going to have to stay here with my mother, aren't I? *You* go. Enjoy your damn self."

Jane's thighs locked with cramp. She adjusted her body

from a crouching to a kneeling position.

She said, "You know I won't go if you don't. What'd be the point? Okay, we'll do something here. What do you want to do tomorrow? Do you go to church?"

"Go out with Gary, damn you. Do you think anyone *wants* you hanging around here?"

Audrey's face, as it thrust itself up from underneath the blankets, was tight and hard with anger.

"Do you think anyone *wants* you lurking around here, stirring up trouble? You *are*, you're a goddamned trouble-maker, do you know that? God, I can't think why I ever asked you to come out with me. Just because your damned mother went and had some sort of miscarriage or something. And stop looking like that. If you want to cry, go and do it in your own room. Go on, get out. Let me get some sleep, will you? Get *out*, Plain."

Jane went.

Picking her sponge bag up from the floor, crossing the carpet, closing the door to Audrey's room behind her, she went.

She didn't want to cry.

Climbing between the cold sheets of her bed, she wanted only to lose consciousness, to drop into a dead and empty sleep, to escape, to forget, to cease to exist.

Lowering her head onto the pillow, seeing the band of yellow that a streetlamp cast across the ceiling, she willed herself not to think. She closed her eyes and heard the strange, unsettling murmur of cars traveling somewhere else through the night. She corkscrewed around onto her stomach and buried her head, her face, her ears, her eyes beneath the pillow.

14

And when she awoke the following morning, it *was* as though something inside her had died. Some nerve, some raw capacity for feeling pain seemed to have been removed from her during the night.

When she joined Mrs. Croft and Audrey in the kitchen for breakfast, when the meal was eaten in silence, when, immediately afterwards, Audrey returned to her bedroom and slammed its door behind her, she felt almost nothing. Nor did she feel either hurt or surprise when Mrs. Croft ignored her offer to help with the washing up.

Enveloped in a thick, humming fog, careless as though with drugs, Jane shrugged, left the kitchen and walked along to the drawing room. She lowered herself onto the chintz-covered sofa. She reached for the pile of magazines that Audrey had discarded the night before.

"... barebacked halter tied under the bosom, with culotte skirt in veils of crepe bias . . ."

The words meant nothing to her, but she gobbled them down. She devoured the glossy photographs: the black-eyed, emaciated women; the stately homes with sloping, crew-cut lawns; the Afghan hounds; the cocktail glasses; the dinner jackets; shoveling them into her emptiness without thought.

It wasn't until the intercom buzzer blared through the flat and she heard Mrs. Croft call out, "Who on *earth* can that be? Baby! Baby, will you answer that? I can't think who on *earth* it can be," that pain flashed back to her. The memory of the night before, Audrey saying, "Go out with Gary, damn you. Do you think anyone *wants* you hanging around here?" licked across Jane's nerve ends like a flame.

She clenched her forehead. The pain withdrew, became dull.

She read ". . . rouleau straps with ruched bodice, £112 . . ."

So long as she could keep still, keep quiet, keep from thinking, then surely everything would be all right.

Audrey's footsteps padded past the closed drawing-room door. The intercom receiver clicked up from its hook.

"Hello? Hello? Oh, it's you, is it?"

There was a second buzz; the sound of the receiver being replaced; the pad, pad, pad of Audrey returning to her room. Jane read the word "diamanté" several times.

"Baby? Darling? Who is it?"

"It's Gary."

"Gareth? What does *he* want?"

"*I* don't know. You'd better ask Jane. She knows all about it."

"Diamanté, diamanté, diamanté," she read.

"What do you mean, I'd better ask Jane? Audrey? Where are you?"

"In my room!"

"There's no need to shout, darling. Did you leave the door open for him?"

"No!"

"What a nuisance that man is."

Jane heard Mrs. Croft leave the kitchen, open the front

door, say, "Oh, hello, this is a bit of a surprise, Gareth. What do you want?"

"Diamanté, diamanté."

"Morning, Mrs. C. I've come to take the girls out for their drive."

"What drive? What are you talking about?"

"I promised I'd take them down to the river. They must've told you. I've got a picnic lunch, all ready, in the car."

"I hope this isn't meant to be a joke, Gareth."

"Most certainly not. Where are they? Young ladies!"

"Audrey! Jane!"

The drawing-room door swept open. As though taken by mild surprise, Jane looked up.

"Hello," she said, smiling, closing the magazine she'd been reading and placing it, carefully, neatly, on the leather-topped table beside her.

"Good morning."

Her face was steady. Her hands were within her control. So long as she could keep them like that, so long as she could remain outside the confusion of anger and questions that swarmed in the drawing-room doorway, she must, surely, be all right. For what could she be blamed, of what could she be accused if she did nothing?

"Jane, what's all this about you arranging to go on a picnic with Gareth? Is it true?"

"Of course it's true. Isn't it, Miss Rackham? Didn't we agree, last night?"

"I wasn't . . ."

"Don't tell me you've changed your mind. I'll be heartbroken."

"Well, I don't think Augy . . ."

"Audrey! Where's she hiding herself? Audrey!"

"Baby!" called Mrs. Croft. "Will you please come here?"

Gary swiveled away from the drawing room and strode to Audrey's bedroom. Jane heard him push open its door.

"What are you hiding in here for, grumpy? Don't you *want* to come for a picnic, then?"

"Of course she doesn't," called Mrs. Croft, leaving the drawing room also. "I don't know *what* can have made you think she would. If *Jane* sees nothing rude in making these alternative arrangements, well, that's entirely up to *her*. If she doesn't think that we're capable of providing the sort of entertainment she's used to . . ."

"All right, Lucrezia."

Gary came back down the hallway. His voice was quieter now, no longer playing.

"Just drop that, will you? It's my fault. There's evidently been a misunderstanding. I'm sorry, Miss Rackham, I should have rung. Maybe some other time, though. Okay?"

He smiled at Jane, his eyebrows drawn, his mouth twisted at one corner as though he would have liked to have said something more. Then he turned to let himself out of the flat.

Jane watched him without emotion, refusing emotion access to her head. She might have been holding her breath under water, so loudly did the blood drum in her ears.

"No, Gary!"

It was Mrs. Croft who spoke.

"No, if you've *promised* to take Jane out, then I think you ought to keep to your word, don't you? After all, it's hardly kind to disappoint a young lady. Look, you can see how much she was looking forward to it."

"Can I?" said Gary, his hand still on the door. "Can I, Miss Rackham? Do you want to come? Even without old Audrey there?"

"Of course she does. Look at her sad little face. Besides, I think, as a matter of fact, it'd be quite a good idea. Don't you, Jane? They think I haven't noticed, but the girls have had a bit of a tiff. Not talking to each other. That sort of thing. Go on, get your coat, Jane. After all, you're going to have to learn to do things without Audrey sometime, aren't you, darling?"

Quite what happened then, Jane wasn't sure. Somehow, she was wearing her coat, was leaving the flat, was descending the stone steps to the street. Gary beside her, she was sitting back in the passenger seat of a sports car. A key was being turned in the ignition lock. The hand brake was being released. The car was being put into gear. The clutch was being lifted. Then, with a roar, with an explosion, the breath that she thought she'd been holding since Gary had arrived at the flat burst free from her. Fresh air flooded her lungs.

What she said, what she did no longer mattered. Gary had taken control. It was his foot on the accelerator pedal that gave her her speed; his wrists, naked where the shirt cuffs fell back from them, that steered her out of the side road, onto High Street, south towards the Thames; his words that supplied her thoughts.

And when, fifteen minutes later, they crossed the river at Putney, swung immediately right, parked the car in front of a deserted boathouse and set out for a walk along the towpath, it was still Gary's words, as much as his arm around her waist, that gave to Jane a direction.

"Forget them, sweetheart," he said, guiding her around a puddle, holding a bramble aside for her to pass. "They're not worth the time of day, believe me. Audrey'll be all right, when you get her back to school this evening. An early night, a few doses of Geography and Latin, she'll be fine. As for Lucrezia, you've just got to feel a bit sorry for her, that's all. Hey! Look! Look there! I bet you don't know what those are."

"What?" said Jane.

"There, on the path ahead. It's a family of lesser spotted heron-coots. Yes, I'm sure it is. How remarkable! They're very rare, you know, heron-coots."

"Those aren't *heron*-coots. They're *ducks*," said Jane, as four of those birds, startled by their approach, lifted themselves from the riverbank and took off in convoy, skimming the gray, rippled water.

"Ducks? Well, maybe you're right. My eyes aren't all that they used to be. Old age . . . Now *that*, now that surely is a swan."

"Fool! It's a man in a boat. It's not your eyes; it's your *brain* that's damaged, if you ask me."

A sculler passed in the opposite direction, his oar slurping, his swift boat skimming the surface of the river.

There were barges anchored midstream, wooden and black and low in the water, and the occasional chugging motorboat rocking the river with its wash.

Once, they passed a trio of boys fishing; once, a black dog, nose to the ground, meandering after a scent.

For the most part, however, they were alone with the wide, quiet flow of the Thames, the smell of mown grass from the fields and commons to their left, the chattering of

103

unseen birds, the ruffle of wind on their faces and in their hair.

"That's *sea* air, you know," said Gary. "Fresh up from the Channel. Breathe, girl. Breathe good and deep."

"I can hardly *help* breathing, you know."

"Now don't make excuses. Got to work up an appetite. In, out. In, out. Come on, I want to hear your lungs *creaking*."

On the tide of his nonsense, he drew her along. His lazy, laughing voice was a life belt that kept her afloat. There were none of the questions or difficult, threatening allusions of the night before; just careless sound and easy, unthinking motion.

They reached the car again as the first, flat drops of a rain shower began to pit the towpath.

Then came food: cheese sandwiches, apples, chocolate digestive biscuits. And wine: a bottle of wine, passed backwards and forwards between them as rain, in sheets now, swept across the gleaming, green hood of the car, swept across the windscreen and beat against the canvas roof.

Then movement once more, the rain stopping, the sun reappearing as Gary pushed the car's roof back, started its engine and sped off westward, out of the town.

"How's that, then?" he shouted. "Fast enough for you?"

They were in the outside lane of a motorway. The cars in the other two lanes, as they passed them, seemed to be standing still, seemed to be slipping backwards, as though trying to drive the wrong way along a giant conveyor belt.

"Yes!" shouted Jane.

She laughed and the sound whipped back past her ears like the flying tails of a scarf. Her eyes watered with the wind that beat against them. Her legs were rigid, thrust against the floor of the car, and her body was clamped to its seat as the speedometer needle touched ninety.

"What happens if the police catch us?" she shouted. "Aren't we breaking some sort of limit or something?"

"What?"

"I said what happens if the police catch us?"

"They won't. They won't be able to."

Gary lowered the toe of his right shoe still farther and the speedometer needle plunged down past ninety to establish itself at ninety-five miles per hour.

"Next stop the Atlantic Ocean!"

"The what?"

"The Atlantic. Fancy a swim, do you?"

Jane said, "Not in *this* weather."

The sky that spanned the valley along whose bed the motorway ran was now a pale, unbroken blue and the fields of grass, rolling away on either side to the horizon, seemed alive with sunlight. But it was March sunlight still, thin and pale and waterlogged.

Twisting herself onto one hip, so that she was half-turned towards Gary, Jane shouted, "You know they'll breathalize us, too, if they catch us. Don't you? Between us, we'd probably make their bags *ignite*."

"On a few sips of wine?"

"We finished the *bottle*. You did, anyway."

"They've still got to catch us first, though, haven't they?"

He smiled and kept the toe of his shoe where it was, as though knowing as well as Jane that she didn't really want him to go slower, would have preferred him, if anything, to have gone faster, to have gone so fast that the road, the fields, the sky might melt together into a white, blinding band.

"You know," she shouted, "I wouldn't mind if we crashed now. I mean, what a way to go! Sort of beating death *to* it. Wham, bang, before it's had time to catch up with you."

Gary laughed, but Jane noticed that he also lightened the pressure of his foot on the accelerator pedal, releasing the speedometer needle to float back up and around, past ninety, past eighty, to seventy-five.

She said, "What are you doing that for?"

"What?"

"Going slower."

"Am I?"

"You know you are. Oh, please, I wasn't being serious. I didn't mean it. Go on, Gary, go faster again."

She watched him. He was still smiling, his eyes narrowed so that the top and bottom lashes met, a small, soft mound at the edge of his lips, but there was something else in his face now, the same sort of seriousness that had been there when he'd talked to her, in the kitchen, the evening before.

Jane felt a spurt of panic.

She'd known, of course, that they couldn't drive on forever, the two of them contained in one car, apart from the rest of the world. Gary had made it seem as though they might, or, rather, had made it seem as though "now" *were* "forever," but she'd known as well as he that it was an illusion. Of course she had.

Only, she couldn't bear it were it to stop just now.

"Please," she said.

"No."

106

"Please. Just a *bit* faster."

"I said *no*."

"I see."

She turned her face away from him, looked down at her legs where they dissolved into shadow beneath the dashboard, fighting, fighting the panic.

"Come on, sweetheart, you're surely not going to sulk because I don't want to kill us both?"

"I'm not *sulking*. It's not *that*."

"What is it then?"

"Nothing. You wouldn't understand," she said, aware that she was being unreasonable, ungracious, yet too busy stifling her fear to stop.

"Okay," said Gary.

Jane clenched her hands. There were bread crumbs lying in her lap. She picked up the largest of these and threw it over her left arm into the car's slipstream. The movement was small enough, but was better than stillness, was better than a stillness in which the panic might return and win.

"It isn't anything. Nothing at all. What *time* is it, anyway?" she asked.

Snaking his fingers around the rim of the steering wheel, never losing contact with it, Gary turned his wrist over.

"Twenty-five past three."

"The school train's at six."

"You think we ought to turn back?"

Gary slowed the car down still more. Glancing up at the driving mirror, he pulled over to the middle lane, then the slow lane. Ahead of them, a large, blue sign announced an exit. He took it.

They crossed the motorway by a bridge and, within less

than half a minute, were heading back the way that they had come, east, towards London, as though they'd never been going anywhere else.

Jane tucked her hands between her thighs. She drew her feet towards her and sat up as straight as she could in the low bucket seat.

Once, she felt Gary turn to look at her. There was a change in the sound of the car engine and the wheels made an almost imperceptible zigzag over the road. But he said nothing.

Only the pleats of the folded-back canvas roof beat with a hollow, clapping sound, only a juggernaut lorry, Milano-Paris-London in red letters on its high, white side, rumbled and swayed to their left.

Then London was all around them: pavements; houses; shops; blocks of flats with children playing football in the courtyards; blocks of blank-windowed Sunday offices; side streets whose narrow mouths pumped forth an endless, senseless flow of cars to join, swell, coarsen and vulgarize *theirs.*

Soon they were hardly moving, the car held up in a clot of traffic so thick that it could only progress a foot or two at a time.

Still saying nothing, keeping his eyes on the road, Gary reached out and took his packet of cheroots from the dashboard. He shook the packet from side to side, creating a panpipe of dark brown-cigarlets, then extracted one and stuck it between his teeth. He took the lighter from his shirt pocket. He closed his mouth and lit the cheroot.

"Miss Rackham?" he said at last, and Jane was shocked by how gentle he sounded, as though he had heard and noted every one of her silent cries.

"Yes?" she said. "What?"

"What who?"

"What, Mr. Clifford."

"That's better. I like a bit of respect from young women. When you reach *my* grotesque age, you know . . ."

He smiled; but a quick, worried smile, without conviction.

Then he said, "Look, sweetheart, about this afternoon . . ."

"What about this afternoon?"

"Look, let's get out of this bloody mess first. Move, you buggers!"

The car's engine strained, then gasped with relief as the traffic surged forwards. They passed a set of green lights, then, almost immediately, swung left and away from the traffic down the narrow, cobbled slope of a cul-de-sac. There, at the bottom of the slope, the car's hood three inches from a pair of closed, royal-blue garage doors, they stopped.

It was suddenly quiet.

Gary opened the ashtray in front of him and tapped the tip of his cheroot against its rim.

"Now, Miss Rackham," he said, taking her chin in his right hand and turning her face towards him.

His hair, where the wind had beat it, stood up from his head in tufts. The skin was tanned on his forehead and on his cheeks. Jane could smell the sweetness of the cheroot around his fingers and feel the in-and-out of his breathing.

"Have we had a good day together?" he asked.

109

"Yes. Of course."

"You've enjoyed yourself?"

"Yes, I said so."

"Okay. Now, tell me, what are you unhappy about?"

Jane pulled her face from his hand.

"Miss Rackham."

"Nothing!" she said. "For goodness' sake, why . . . ? Why don't you just take me back to the flat, if you're going to?"

"There's plenty of time," said Gary.

Jane pivoted around in her seat. She plowed one finger along the rubber sill of the passenger window. She turned the finger over. It was clean.

"I shouldn't ever've come out with you in the first place," she said.

She rubbed the clean finger hard against her thigh, back and forwards, back and forwards, until it burned with the friction.

"Oh? Why's that?" asked Gary.

"I just shouldn't have."

"But I thought you said you'd enjoyed yourself. Didn't you? *I* certainly did."

"*Yes.* I *did.* But don't you understand? I've got to go *back* now. And Augy's going to be furious and . . . Don't you see? The whole weekend's been ruined."

"No. I don't see. Look, look, Miss Rackham, if you'd stayed at the flat this morning, what kind of a day do you think you'd've had? Awful! Wouldn't it have been?"

"I don't know."

"Of course you do. How was it, before I turned up to take you out?"

Still three-quarters turned away from him, Jane

110

shrugged. She pulled at the rubber strip beneath the car's window and a shred came away in her hand. She dropped it to the floor.

"Exactly," said Gary. "And maybe it wasn't such a bad thing, either, for Audrey and her mum to be alone together for a bit. Maybe they needed it. So . . ."

"You don't know what she said to me, do you, last night?"

"Who?" asked Gary, extinguishing his cheroot.

"Augy. She said, 'Do you think anyone *wants* you hanging around here?' I mean . . . I mean, it's not *my* fault. *I* couldn't help it if her mother was cross about the bracelet, could I? Why did she have to take it out on *me*?"

"Well, who else?"

"What do you mean?"

"Who else *could* she have taken it out on? Besides, you must see it from her point of view. Think how embarrassed *you*'d be if your mother'd behaved like Lucrezia did last night, in front of your best friend. It can't have been easy. How would you have reacted?"

"I wouldn't have . . . Well, she shouldn't have asked me out, then."

"Now that's just stupid."

"No it isn't."

"Jane! Miss Rackham, look, come here, before you finish pulling my car to pieces."

Gary grabbed Jane's hands in his and drew her around to face him.

"Now listen," he said, "it may have escaped your notice, but I like you, Jane. I like you a lot. . . . No, please, shh, don't wriggle. I'm not going to tell you you've got beautiful eyes again. Nothing like that. Okay? No, why I like you is because you're intelligent and you're sensitive and you're angry. All fine things to be.

"But they can be frightening, too, can't they? And confusing. All those questions you can't help beginning to ask, all those things you can't help sensing. Mysteries, depths that you hadn't suspected, *dangers* you hadn't suspected, doubts . . . They *are* frightening, aren't they? Of course they are. I do know just how you feel. But, you see, the thing is, you can't get rid of fear by blocking your ears and eyes and screaming for someone to come and tell you it's all all right. Maybe you could once, but you're too old now. It's time to learn to cope with the dark yourself, to look at it, look *into* it and see just exactly what's there. That's the only way you'll ever understand it, the only way you'll stop being afraid. Do you think you know what I'm saying?"

"Yes. Yes, I think so," said Jane, but her attention was focused elsewhere, was focused down to where Gary's hands held hers, to where Gary's strong, hard fingers enclosed her soft ones and she'd scarcely heard one word that he had said.

"Do you?" asked Gary. "Then do you also see how unhelpful it is to blame Audrey, or Lucrezia, or even me, for whatever it is you think's gone wrong this weekend? Not un*fair.* Just unhelpful. Because, by blaming everyone else, what you're really doing is putting your life in everyone else's power. Do you see? And, as long as you do that, you'll never be able to conquer fear for yourself. You'll always be vulnerable, confused. You'll always be on the run. Is any of this making sense, Miss Rackham?"

"I suppose so," said Jane, but she was still watching his

hands around hers, was still being bathed by the wave upon wave of peace that his low voice poured into her. His smell, of lemons and of cheroot smoke, was lapping her brain. His concern was enveloping her.

"Well," said Gary.

Then Jane heard him laugh.

"Good heavens, what a solemn, serious way to end the day!"

He let her go. He reached for the packet of cheroots that was lying on the dashboard.

"I feel like a priest or something. Don't you think so? Don't you think I sound a bit like a priest?"

"No," said Jane, looking up at him, seeing his smile and catching it, involuntarily, in her eyes.

"Don't you?" he asked. "Not a bit! Not with all those noble exhortations for the good of your soul?"

"No. If you'd seen our school vicar, you'd know he wasn't in the least bit noble. He even cleans his ears out with his little fingers when he's giving a sermon."

"Does he? How extraordinarily unattractive."

"Yes, isn't it? I mean, can you imagine, if we were Catholics and then had to go and kiss his hand or something?"

"No! Please! Miss Rackham!"

Jane laughed. Gary laughed. Beyond the windscreen of the car, a sprig of yellow forsythia rattled against the closed garage doors in front of which they were parked.

Gary lit a cheroot, replaced the packet on the dashboard and then, in a continuation of the same movement, reached for the square, silver key in the ignition lock.

He turned it.

Jane's throat tightened around her laughter.

But Gary was saying, "You've got a *repulsive* imagination, do you know that, Miss Rackham? Is this the same poor vicar you supposed would have to lick up the communion wine the cat spilled?"

"Yes," said Jane and her laughter returned, strong, because Gary remembered the story and had liked it.

But there was something else, something more that she wanted, needed, as the car's engine caught and the clutch was depressed to the floor.

"Gary?"

"Yes, my sweetheart."

The gears had been slid into reverse. The car was backing up the cobbled slope of the cul-de-sac.

"About . . ." said Jane. "You know. I mean, about Augy. I still think she's going to be cross that I went out with you today."

"Do you?"

"Yes."

The car edged backwards onto the main road, feeding itself into gaps in the oncoming traffic.

"But you'll be able to cope with it now, won't you?" asked Gary. "Understanding that it's not all her fault, that she's just upset about Lucrezia making a fool of her?"

"Yes, I know that. But . . ."

The car had stopped, but its engine continued to strain, awaiting the chance to spring forward.

"I just don't know if . . . I mean, it's all right when you're talking about it, but. . . ."

"Listen," said Gary. "We're friends, aren't we? So, if you find you're having problems, about anything, I mean, then you must simply tell me."

"How *can* I?"

"You can write, can't you? Or even telephone. Audrey seems to telephone Henny whenever she feels like it."

"Do you mean that?"

"Of course. Why shouldn't I? I did mean what I said to you before, you know."

"Oh, that's . . . !"

As the car leaped into a space in the stream of traffic, Jane discovered that she was smiling again, that her face and her head and her heart were electric with pleasure. Precisely what it was that Gary'd been referring to, by the words, "I did mean what I said to you before," she didn't know; nor did she care. All that mattered was that his concern for her would continue when the drive was over, would still be there for her to touch, to cling to, when their day together was ended.

"Little idiot," said Gary, stretching out to ruffle her hair as Jane's pleasure exploded, beyond a smile, into new, uncontrollable laughter.

Part 4

15

He left her on the pavement outside the Crofts' flat at a quarter past five. He drove away before she'd reached the top step, before she'd sounded the intercom, but Jane had his words, his promise, as the buzzer buzzed and the thick double doors swung open before her thrust.

On reaching Flat J, she had at once to wash her hands, brush her hair, lock her suitcase and hurry back down to the street where, already, Mrs. Croft, Audrey and a meter-ticking taxi awaited her.

The drive to the station was silent. But still Jane had Gary's promise.

On the train, both Audrey and she were immediately surrounded by the same group of girls as those with whom they'd traveled up the day before; all excited and shouting and handing around packets of sweets. Their escort, this time, wasn't the Haggis, but an elderly woman called Mrs. Baker, who taught History.

As the train pulled out of the station, she clapped together

her tiny, molelike hands and cried, "Please, my dears, be quiet! I have to tell you that nobody's to leave the carriage, except one at a time. It's because of the silly way that some of you behaved on Saturday. I'm sorry, but let's buckle down and see if we can't make up for it now, shall we?"

Without thinking, Jane leaned across the aisle to Audrey, touched Audrey's leg and smiled. But the other only turned her eyes to a window and rolled her shoulders in a gesture of bored rejection.

At once, Jane dived back inside her own head, found Gary's words, "You can write, can't you? Or telephone," and enmeshed herself safely among them.

A fourth-former shook a bag of peanut brittle beneath her nose.

She accepted a piece.

Someone told a joke that her older brother had told her.

"Please, dears, do try and be a little less noisy," cried Mrs. Baker.

Someone else, a first-former with short, red hair and protruding front teeth, tried to climb onto the luggage rack without Mrs. Baker's noticing.

"Beverly, don't do that, you might hurt yourself."

The noise, the movement, the energy in the railway carriage surrounded Jane's thoughts like a blanket, preserving them, protecting them from intrusion.

They reached their station at a quarter past seven.

Then came the numbing debilitation of the final stage in the return to school: the drive through dusk in the minibus; the gossip fading into silence as the various countdown landmarks, the village store, the village church, the telephone kiosk on its triangular island of grass at the far end of the village, Eliston's Woods and the white, wooden gate-posts of the school grounds were each in turn passed; the crunch of gravel beneath the wheels of the minibus as it circled, then drew up, before the school's open front door; the smell, forgotten, but at once familiar, of floor polish and overcooked cabbage; the cracked clanking of a handbell down a long corridor, announcing that it was time for the evening meal.

Supper. Chapel. Bed.

Chapel. Breakfast. Assembly.

The first lesson of the morning.

Through it all, Jane remained submerged inside herself, allowing her body to float on the omnipotent tide of the school timetable, but clinging, with her thoughts, to the anchor of Gary's voice inside her head.

It wasn't until halfway through that first Monday morning lesson, when, lifting the lid of her desk to get out her copy of *Julius Caesar*, she noticed that Audrey was leaning forward to tap Nicky Lawrence, with a ruler, between the shoulder blades, that the reality of the present smacked her mind from its mooring. With a shock that was almost physical, that almost made her gasp, Jane's perception broke free from the quiet, cheroot-scented warmth of the previous afternoon to focus on the fifth-form classroom.

The lid of her desk propped open upon her left forearm, her right-hand fingers thrust among a mess of textbooks and exercise books, she saw, with extreme clarity, Nicky turn, smile at Audrey and tilt back towards her on her chair.

What was happening? What was going on? If Audrey had something to say, some comment to make on the lesson, it was always to *Jane* that she said it.

"Nicola! Audrey!"

Nicola and Audrey? It was always "Audrey! Jane!"

"What do you two suppose you're doing? I thought I told you to read through Act Five, in silence. Not *whisper* to each other."

"Sorry, Miss Rendei."

"Sorry, Miss Rendel."

Jane snapped her eyes back to her desk. She found the copy of *Julius Caesar*. She extracted it and closed the desk's lid.

"Damn her!" she shouted inside her head.

She'd been right, then. Why hadn't Gary believed her? Why hadn't he taken her seriously, when she'd said that Audrey'd be cross? It was all very well to say she must understand *why*, but understanding didn't change anything, did it? It wasn't preventing Audrey from ignoring her, from whispering to Nicky instead.

Suddenly, the magic of Gary's promise, the spell of his low, singing voice seemed impotent. What good did it do, after all, to remember that he'd said, "I like you, Jane," to repeat, like a prayer, "You can write, can't you? Or even telephone"?

None. Not here. Not in the long fifth-form classroom, with its smells of bitter ink and of plaster, with its sounds of rustling paper and restless feet. This was a world immune from the larger one that contained it and, for those who lived in it, more real.

Even had Jane been *able* to rush from the room, to run to the village coin box and call him, what could Gary have done? How could he even know what it *meant*, that Audrey had chosen to whisper to Nicky and not to her? He couldn't. He couldn't. Whatever he'd promised, he couldn't.

"Jane Rackham!"

"Yes?"

She struggled to focus on the place where the voice had come from, on Miss Rendel leaning forwards across the high staff desk.

"Yes? Just yes? Is that all you've got to say, yes? You're supposed to be reading Act Five of *Julius Caesar*, not going to sleep. Or do you know the play by heart? Is that what it is? Because, if so, I'd be fascinated to hear it. We all should be."

The class laughed. Jane listened for Audrey's laughter among the rest, but couldn't find it.

She said, "I'm sorry, I wasn't thinking."

"Then you'd better start, hadn't you? In case you'd forgotten, you have an exam in one week's time. Of course, I appreciate that, for someone as brilliant as you, it isn't actually necessary to *read* a play before answering questions on it, but you might at least pretend, so as not to make the rest of us feel *too* inferior."

This time, Audrey also laughed. Jane heard the sound, hard, staccato and repressed, vicious among the easy amusement of the others, as though it were a tactile thing, as though it were jabbing, jabbing, just out of sight, at her head.

Stomach thudding, mouth dry, she opened her book to Act Five.

"All right, silence please, silence. This isn't the cinema. Now, since obviously none of you is capable of reading to

123

yourselves, we'd better have it out loud. Like babies. Nicola, will you read Octavius? Anthony, Miranda. Messenger . . . Who'll do the messenger? Thank you, Loretta. I suppose you'd better be Brutus, Jane, that's if you're sure you won't find it too boring. Cassius, Audrey . . ."

After English, a break for biscuits and milk. After the break, History. After History, French.

An inexorable wave, the timetable rolled on, carrying pupils and staff, alike, like flotsam on its broad back. Jane, too, moved with it, but, for the first time in her life, was aware of an effort in doing so, a conscious impression of struggling to keep afloat. It was ridiculous. For the last four and a half years, she'd followed its pull with the ease that comes from knowing there to be no alternative. It had been her element, her motor, her justification for everything she did. Now, suddenly, it was as though not just Audrey, but the whole school, its rules and rituals and values, were rejecting her. She felt apart from them, divorced, and couldn't understand why. She began to feel frightened.

After French, came lunch.

The dining-room rota, designed to ensure that no girl sat at the same table, or with the same people, two weeks running, had removed Jane from the company of Loretta van Straten and Nicky Lawrence and given her that of Ruth Bottomly instead. Ruth never spoke while eating. The other girls at Jane's end of the table were from junior forms to hers and unlikely, therefore, to address her with anything but requests for salt, water, or bread.

Thus, immured by silence, a silence made only more solid by the hum of voices, the tinkle of cutlery, the squeaking of chair legs that defined it, Jane tried to concentrate on the food in front of her: corned beef fritters, chips and peas, her favorite Monday lunch. Today, however, it tasted of nothing. She ate it all, she accepted a second helping, but her hunger remained unsatisfied. No, not her hunger. Her need. Her need for someone or something to say, "It's all right. Whatever you've done, whatever you did this weekend, we accept you back. You still belong."

"Ruth?" she said abruptly.

But Ruth Bottomly, her thick, black fringe almost brushing the top of the table, was scraping the last of some chocolate sauce from a pudding bowl and didn't answer.

"She's got this great, fat face, with black eyebrows and a black mustache. . . ."

Why had Jane said that? To make Gary laugh?

And had he?

Jane couldn't remember. As the present remained beyond her reach, so also the past was withdrawing. She was alone between the two of them; as Miss Anthony, supervising the meal from the top table, rang the small, brass handbell in the shape of a shepherdess and called for silence, grace, the end of lunch.

16

What increased Jane's feeling of aloneness, as the afternoon began to unfold with the same inevitability as had the morning, was the fact that no one but she seemed aware of it. In the eyes that met hers, there was no astonishment. Nor was there any pity, or scorn, or alarm in the voices that persisted in addressing her.

"Plain, can you lend me a piece of blotting paper? Some creep's gone and nicked all of mine."

"Have you written that thing we were supposed to do for the Termite, yet, Plain?"

Her friends spoke just as though nothing had happened, as though they were deaf to the effort it cost her both to hear them and to reply.

As for Audrey, she maintained a distance that precluded confrontation; not obviously cutting Jane, just avoiding the need to do so. All through the Termite's Civics lesson, all through the games period afterwards, she kept, without apparent deliberation, an uncrossable space between them. Jane's nerves began to scream with the tension. She knew that she was right, that Audrey *was* avoiding her, but she needed some loud, unmistakable proof, something that couldn't, afterwards, be denied.

"Hurry up, girls, hurry up. You'll be late for tea. Get a move on there. Hurry up."

"Shut up, Haggis, shut up," said Miranda Spurling, on the same whistle-shrill monotone, but quietly enough for the games mistress not to hear her. Then she smiled at Jane her Cheshire cat grin, because mimicking the Haggis was known to be Plain's speciality.

Looking up from a knot in the lace of one of her lacrosse boots, Jane smiled back; a meaningless smile, her attention being focused somewhere else in the changing room, to her left, where Audrey and Nicky Lawrence were talking.

"Hey, Plain, did you have a good weekend out? With Augy?"

126

"What?" said Jane, becoming once more aware of Miranda's round, freckled face. "Oh, yes. Yeah. It was fine."

"What did you do? Did you meet her sister?"

"Yes."

"Is she nice?"

"Yes, of course."

"What about her husband? Is it true he writes plays?"

"Oh, for goodness' sake, Randy!"

"Sorry. Sorry. What's the matter?"

"Nothing," said Jane. "I . . . Nothing."

If she was ashamed of having shouted at Miranda, whose buoyant good nature and cheerfulness made her the most liked girl in the class, she was more concerned to overhear what Nicky was now whispering to Audrey. What *was* it? It sounded like her own name, repeated again and again. Not "Plain," but "Jane Rackham," as though it were a joke.

She stood up, one foot still clothed, the other naked on the cold, gritty linoleum. She looked at them.

Audrey had her back to her. Nicky was facing in her direction, but looking at Audrey, smiling. They stood close together. When they laughed, as now they did, their foreheads bumped and they gripped one another's arms.

Then, from the cuff of Audrey's left shirt sleeve, Jane saw flash out a sliver of silver light, a ripple of silver links that made a soft ringing sound. She saw Audrey glance at her wrist, saw Nicky glance, too; then saw Nicky touch the white metal, look up at Audrey and smile.

"Audrey!"

She was surprised at how easily the word came out, how

clear and strong it sounded now that, at last, it was unavoidable.

What she couldn't quite understand was why everybody along the alleyway stopped talking, turned to watch her. She knew that she hadn't shouted.

"Audrey!"

"I believe somebody wants to talk to you," said Nicky Lawrence, her slim eyebrows more arched than usual, her top lip hitched into a half smile. Jane hadn't noticed before how ugly she was, how the sneer that she always wore had scarred her mouth, puckered it, as though with dead skin tissue.

She said, "Yes, just Audrey. Not you, thanks a lot, Nicky."

Somebody sniggered, a stupid, nervous sound.

Audrey said, "For goodness' sake . . ."

"Come along, girls, hurry up. Look, there's some of you not even undressed yet. Get a move on, Jane Rackham. It'll be teatime in a moment."

Jane waited, motionless, until Miss MacKenzie's voice had passed on to the neighboring alleyway, then said, "Do you mind, Audrey?"

"What on earth are you playing at now?" asked Audrey.

"I should say she was in some sort of a tizzy about something, wouldn't you?" said Nicky.

Jane sighed. Nicky was only trying to be amusing, to earn a cheap laugh.

If she succeeded, it wasn't because there was any truth in her conjecture, it was merely because the others were relieved that she wasn't sharpening her tongue on them. Her own voice, she knew, was betraying no fear. She could hear it as though it belonged to somebody else.

"Listen, Nicky, no one cares a damn what you 'should say' or what you shouldn't, so just shut up, will you? Augy?"

Audrey shut the door of her locker.

She said, "I don't know what you're on about."

She began to move towards Jane, towards the changing-room exit. Jane took a step to her right and blocked the passage. From around them came the soft inrush of breath.

"Oh, look, why don't the rest of you go and get your tea, instead of gooping about like morons?" said Jane. "Augy, I just think we ought to talk, that's all. In private. Please?"

There was no appeal in that last word. Jane was delighted at how matter-of-fact it came out, more like a statement than a question. Audrey's unease as she stood there, trapped, her face hot and red, her lips locked, her dark eyes trying to glare a tunnel through Jane's face, also delighted her. About what was now taking place there was something so strong, so inevitable, that she felt the need to do nothing but relax and enjoy it.

"You *know* what about, don't you?" she said. "I mean, you don't want everybody listening in, or do you?"

"Piss off, Jane Rackham."

Jane laughed.

"What's the matter, Augy? I just thought we ought to talk. What are you frightened of? I'm not going to say anything about your mother."

The thrust against her forehead came so hard that she had to take two steps backwards. The rubber studs of her one lacrosse boot stuck on the surface of the linoleum. She lost her balance. Her legs buckled. She crashed against a locker and slid, bare arm scraping metal, to the floor.

She closed her eyes.

She waited for the winded feeling to pass and the sickness from the jolt to her coccyx. As soon as these had begun to recede, she opened her eyes, shook the hair from her face and got up. Audrey had gone.

The others, Nicky Lawrence included, stood just as they had before she'd fallen, their bodies frozen at that moment when relaxation stiffens into movement, but hasn't yet decided in which direction to go, their faces blank, stupid, waiting.

"What's going on down there?" called Miss MacKenzie.

"Nothing," said Jane.

To Nicky, she said, "What's the matter with *you*? Shouldn't you be with your friend?"

Nicky shrugged, put the weight onto her forward foot, stopped and said, "You okay?"

"Fine, thanks. I'm sorry. Next time I'll try to break my neck or something."

"Yes. Well maybe that wouldn't be such a terrible idea."

Nicky went. But the others, Miranda, Simone de Preville, Loretta van Straten, Rose Mercer and a girl called Fiona who was new to the school that year, shuffled, still waiting for a direction.

"Well, what are you looking at?" asked Jane, aware that her voice was weakening, was beginning to crack. For heaven's sake, what more did they want from her? She'd clarified the situation, hadn't she? What more did they expect?

"Are you sure you don't want to sit down or something?" asked Miranda, after a moment.

Loretta said, "You do look a bit strange, Plain. Your face is all white. I think you're going to faint."

"I'm perfectly all right, thank you," said Jane.

She lifted the foot which still had its boot on and propped it against the knee of her other, supporting leg. She bent from the waist to untie the lace. She slipped the boot off, slipped the woolen games sock off, straightened up and threw both garments into her locker.

"Aren't you going to tell us what all that was about, then?" asked Rose, her sharp, sallow face as keen as a weasel's.

"Have you and Augy had a row or something?" asked Miranda.

"You should've seen her face just before she hit you," said Rose. "I thought she was going to explode."

Their eagerness wasn't only for information, but for clues from Jane's voice, from her attitude, as to how they should behave, as to whose side they should take in the pending hostilities. But couldn't they see that it wasn't a question of Jane versus Audrey and Nicky, but of Jane against the whole school? She'd become an outcast. Somehow, the weekend had made her an exile. Why were they taking so long to understand?

Her pink face as greedy for scandal as it was for biscuits and sweets, Loretta said, "What were you getting at her about? You know, at Augy? What was all that about her mother?"

Jane removed her Aertex shirt. She replaced it with her white Viyella shirt, her tie and her blue sweater. She unbuttoned her shorts.

"Why didn't you want anyone else to hear?"

"Did you have a row over the weekend or something?"

"Look, it's nothing to do with you. With *any* of you," Jane said, as her shorts slithered to the floor.

"Oh, I see."

"Be like that then."

"Yes," she said, "I shall be like that. Thanks for your permission."

"Come on, what's *wrong* with you?"

"Nothing."

She could feel that they were becoming restless and was glad.

"Nothing's wrong with *me*, thanks," she said.

"Well, it certainly looks as though something is."

"Doesn't it."

"And what were you getting at Nicky for? What's she supposed to have done?"

"Look, are you sure you didn't hurt yourself?"

"What was the row *about*?"

"Are you sure Augy didn't hurt you, Plain? You went down with quite a thump."

In spite of everything, they were still uncertain, vacillating. Curiosity, and a natural sympathy for the victim of physical violence, held them in its balance.

Then the tea bell rang.

Clang-kerdy-clang-kerdy-clang-kerdy. It was shaken at the top of the basement steps, its cry pervading the changing room before fading away to stir some other part of the school.

"Come on."

They began to move, to close their locker doors, to tuck their shirts in.

132

"If *she* wants to stay here sulking, that's *her* business."

"Hurry up, or there won't be any cakes left."

"You'd better hurry, Plain."

"Come on."

Like an army in shameful retreat, their bodies twisted, ill at ease with the way in which their feet were leading them, they began to desert the changing room. From the doorway, Miss MacKenzie's cries encouraged them.

"That's right, that's right, look lively now. I've never known girls as slow as you. Everybody out now? Come on. Quick, quick. That's right."

Their footsteps accelerated up the wooden staircase.

Jane was alone.

The muffled drumming on the basement ceiling, caused by the tramp of feet through the dining room above, continued for a second or two, then stumbled into silence.

"One," counted Jane, "two . . ."

A prefect would be reciting the abbreviated teatime grace: "For what we are about to receive, may the Lord make us truly thankful."

". . . three!"

Chair legs clattered and banged and screeched across polished wood. Eighty-nine voices bubbled again into life, became one voice, the loud, excited, particular voice of the school sitting down to tea. Knowing so well how it would be up there, how it would smell, what it would look like, what kind of cakes (sponge topped with jam and shredded coconut) they would be eating, Jane was half-surprised to remember that her body was still down here, standing clothed, but barefooted, in a deserted alleyway of the gloomy, chill and sweat-stale basement.

133

Yet she made no attempt to move it.

It was done, then. The confirmation that she'd wanted, all day, of her isolation was now complete.

She wriggled her right hand up the left sleeve of her shirt to feel the raw, swollen place where she'd scraped her arm on a locker handle in falling. It was hot. Her fingers cooled it.

There was nothing more she could lose. She'd lost everything.

She reached up to the top shelf of her locker for her tights. As she pulled them towards her, a sheet of white paper slid with them and fell, turning once, to the floor. Puzzled, she bent to pick it up. It was an envelope, its top edge torn, the address neat, rectangular and typewritten. She remembered.

At once, she thrust the envelope back from whence it had come, buried it under a pile of clothes, made it invisible. She didn't want *that*, not *now*.

"Now THERE IS NOTHING FOR YOU TO WORRY ABOUT," it had said.

Well then, fine, she wouldn't. If they were all so happy without her . . . What did they care . . . ? No, what did *she* care?

Face clenched, fists clenched, Jane strode backwards and forwards along the empty alleyway, trying to forget the envelope, trying, also, to forget the look that had flared across Audrey's face just before she had hit her.

"Gary," she thought.

That was better.

"Gary."

What was it? What was it he'd said?

"I like you, Jane. I like you a lot."

And his car, like the hand of a giant, had lifted her up, had carried her away from that awful morning with the Crofts, had enclosed her and borne her and sustained her. . . .

"So if you find you're having problems, about anything, I mean, then you must simply tell me."

"How *can* I?" she'd said.

"You can write, can't you?" he'd answered. "Or even telephone."

17

"Gary. Gary. Gary. Gary."

Through prep time, through supper, through free time, through the night, Jane's blood beat to his name.

Waking the following morning, she listened for it before opening her eyes and still it was there.

"Gary."

"Morning, Plain," said Rose, her small eyes narrowed and cautious.

"Morning, Plain," said Loretta, brushing her spun-gold hair.

Hearing their voices like oil drops on the surface of her thoughts, Jane only nodded.

"Good gracious, Plain, what on earth have you done to your arm? It's all swollen and scraped," said Ruth Bottomly, as her large, red face emerged through the neck of her sweater.

Jane didn't answer. Rose and Loretta frowned at Ruth,

made warning signs with their mouths.

Along the dormitory corridor swelled the under-matron's call.

"Hurry up. Who's not dressed yet? Chapel in a minute. Hurry up."

"Gary," beat the pulse in Jane's forehead. "Gary. Gary. Gary."

Approximately five hours later, the morning's lessons done, lunch eaten, letters distributed, the fifth form trooped down the basement stairs to get changed for another lacrosse game. As far as the changing-room door, Jane followed them. Then she stopped, dug one hand into the pocket of her skirt as though looking for something, waited until the stragglers had passed her, swiveled around on her toes and ran back up the wooden stairs to the ground floor, then up another flight to the first.

As she reached the staff room, the Haggis, wearing a roll-neck sweater and wide, loose shorts, was leaving it.

"Jane Rackham?" she said. "What are *you* doing here? Aren't you supposed to be getting ready for games?"

"Please, Miss MacKenzie, I wonder if I could be excused."

"What on earth for?"

"I'm afraid I've just started a rather bad period," said Jane. "I'm feeling awful. Honestly. I think I'm going to be sick or something."

"Have you told matron?"

"I'm just about to."

"Well . . ."

The Haggis fiddled with the whistle that hung from a ribbon around her neck.

"Well," she said, "I suppose . . . It would do you *good*, though, you know, a wee run around."

"I couldn't. Really. I feel . . ."

Jane closed her eyes and shivered. She opened her eyes and smiled as though to do so were an effort.

"Really, I don't think . . . I do feel very sick," she said, impatience ticking inside her like a time bomb. "If I could just lie down for an hour or two, I'm sure I'll feel better. It's happened before."

"Well, if you think so, though I'm sure a bit of fresh air would do you much more good. But you will report to matron, won't you? I'll be checking up to see that you have. You're getting a bit disobedient these days, Jane. A bit ill-mannered. Your behavior on the train on Saturday wasn't worthy of you. I've had to tell Miss Anthony about that, I'm afraid."

"Yes, I'm sorry," said Jane.

"Off you go, then."

"Thank you."

Jane started back the way that she had come, towards the pupils' staircase. But when she reached the end of the corridor, instead of climbing up to the second floor to find the matron, she stopped and held her breath, listening to the sound of the Haggis's rubber-soled footsteps as they changed, from a squeaking against linoleum, to a *slap, slap, slap* on the marble steps of the wide, curving staff stairs.

When, at last, even by straining, she could no longer hear them, Jane returned her focus to the place where she was and began to count up to twenty; then up to thirty, just in case.

Above her and below her, the school was as quiet as a building that isn't empty can be. The senior girls would be

137

on their way up the drive to the games fields. The juniors would be in their classrooms. Those members of the staff who weren't taking a lesson would have gone, either home, or, if living in, to their rooms on the topmost floor; or be drinking after-lunch coffee in the staff room. The maids would be in the kitchen, washing up.

Fingertips resting on the banister as though for support, as though to diminish her weight on the ill-fitted boards, Jane began to descend the wooden staircase.

She reached the ground floor. To her left was the entrance to the basement. To her right, the glass-domed hall.

She turned right.

Beside the hexagonal table that stood in the middle of the hall, in a splash of warm sunlight on the tiled floor, lay the Termite's black-and-white kitten. Hearing Jane approach, he contracted his elongated body and sprang to his feet.

Jane stopped a few yards from him.

The kitten sat back on his haunches. He twisted his head around through forty-five degrees and began to lick his neck, his sharp, rough, pink tongue burrowing deep into the pile of his fur.

Jane began once more to move.

The kitten stopped cleaning himself, looked at her and gave an indignant, petulant squawk. It wasn't a loud sound, but it pricked Jane's skin with sweat. Whether or not she got into trouble *later* was irrelevant to her, but she mustn't be stopped *now*.

She listened. There was no movement from the Termite's study on the far side of the hall and, from the school office, only the steady, muffled ticking of a typewriter. She frowned at the kitten, willing him to be quiet, yet knowing the absurdity of willing a cat to do anything.

"Shhh," she mouthed.

The kitten squawked again, then stood up and strolled towards her, rubbed the side of his head against her leg. At once, Jane bent to knead the hollow behind his left ear. The gesture was so familiar that it performed itself. But before the soft rumblings in the kitten's throat had had time to accelerate into a purr, Jane snatched her hand back and straightened up, anger tightening her chest, a feeling of having almost been betrayed.

"Go on, get off," she said, loudly enough for the cat to hear the anger, then she turned away from him, walked to the front door, stepped out onto the gravel, closed the door behind her and set off up the drive.

As she walked, she could hear the screams and shouts of the lacrosse players borne in faint gusts on the breeze, but long before she reached the turnstile that led to the games fields, she turned to her right and climbed the fence on the other side of the drive, into a sheep field. There, she followed a footpath that undulated with the dip and rise of the land, but, nonetheless, cut straight across the field to the band of dark trees on the skyline: Eliston's Woods.

Striding as fast as she could without breaking into a trot, her nostrils straining for air, Jane knew that with every step that she took away from the school drive she was increasing her chances of being spotted; from a top-floor window, maybe; from the games fields, now that she was reaching higher ground. But every step was also taking her farther away from recapture, was also taking her closer to her goal.

It was approximately half an hour later that she reached the telephone kiosk that stood on a triangle of grass, at a

T junction, on the outskirts of the village.

There, she quickly found the directory marked "London Postal Area, A–D."

Clifford.

Clifford, A.; Clifford, David; Clifford, E.M. . . .

Jane's hands were clumsy, holding the soft, heavy book, and her attention kept jumping away from the page, as a car passed, as an old woman, with an old, fat dog at her heels, passed, then turned back to look at her.

Clifford, G.

But an address in North East London.

Clifford, Gareth.

She'd found it. She'd found his name. Camouflaged among all the other meaningless, gray letters, she'd found his name. And these, then, these seven figures divided into two groups, one of three, one of four, must be his telephone number. She had only to dial the London code, followed by these seven numbers, and she'd hear his voice.

Jane didn't doubt that Gary would answer. In a room lined with bookcases, with a desk facing two large sash windows to the street, a typewriter in front of him, a telephone within reach, he must be half expecting to hear from her. That Henrietta might also be at home, that she might not work on a Tuesday, was immaterial. It would be Gary who would answer.

Jane began to dial: zero, one, nine . . .

The disk sprang away from the pressure of her finger and she had to begin again.

Zero, one, nine, three, seven . . .

There was a short pause after she'd finished dialing, then a hollow, intermittent death rattle, indicating that the line

140

was free, then a click, then an hysterical ticking. Jane pushed some coins into a slot. The ticking stopped.

A voice said, "Hello? Aberystwyth dry cleaners and funeral parlor."

"What? I . . ."

"Who's speaking?"

"What? I wanted . . ."

"Hello, who *is* that?"

"My name's Jane Rackham. I wanted . . ."

"Good heavens. Miss Rackham? I don't believe it. This is Gary. What a surprise to hear from you. I thought you were the Inland Revenue, or the Electricity Board, hounding me for money. How are you? To what do I owe this overwhelming honor? Are you well?"

"Yes. Fine," said Jane.

Suddenly, she felt cold, shivery, bewildered, as though she'd been woken up, with a start, in a room that she didn't know. What was she doing? To whom was she speaking? Wasn't something supposed to happen now?

"Good," said the voice in her right ear, a voice that could have been anyone's. "How very lovely to hear from you. I assume you got back to school all right and so on."

"Yes," she said. "Fine."

"Good."

"I . . . I just . . ."

She reached forward and stroked the wall of the kiosk, once, with her free fingertips.

"Well," said the voice in her right ear.

The shivering inside her grew tighter, faster. She pressed the wall with her fingertips until they turned a pale yellow. She clenched her jaw.

"Well, what have you been up to, then, since Sunday?"

The shivering was becoming uncontrollable. She could see it, now, in her hands and in her forearms, could feel it in her back and the back of her legs.

"I should be playing lacrosse," she said, not knowing what she meant.

"Sorry? I didn't . . ."

She thrust her lips inside the cup of the receiver.

"I shouldn't *be* here. I should be playing *lacrosse*."

"Hey, sweetheart, what is it?"

"*Lacrosse* I told you."

"All right, I know, I heard. Jane, Miss Rackham, what's up?"

"What's up? You told me to *ring* you, didn't you? Didn't you tell me to ring you? Isn't that . . . ? Isn't that . . . ? Isn't that what you *said*?"

Her jaw was clattering. How could he hear her, how could *anyone*'ve heard her, above the noise it was making?

"Yes. Yes, it is," said the voice. "I *did* say you could ring me. But . . . Jane, please. *Please*. Please, try and be a bit calmer. I can't understand what you're saying. What's *happened*? Just tell me what's happened."

"Then why did you *say* it?" asked Jane.

"What? That you could ring me? Because you *can*. Because I *meant* it. So . . . Look, look, what is it? Is it Audrey? Is it something to do with Audrey?"

"Where *are* you?" asked Jane.

"Here. I'm at home. I'm in London. . . . Jane, please! For God's . . . Sweetheart, it's no good shouting like that. I can't make head nor tail. . . . Jane, listen, are you alone?"

"Yes!"

"Okay. All right. Now, where are *you*?"

"What?"

"Can you tell me where *you* are?"

"I'm . . ."

Jane tried to rotate her head, but the shivering seemed to impede her, like a counterforce.

"Where *are* you? You're in a telephone box. All right. Now, where? Not in the school, obviously."

"No," said Jane.

"Then where? Come on, sweetheart, pull yourself together. I've got to know. Are you near a village?"

"Yes. The village."

"*The* village. Where the station is. Okay, fine, I can look it up on a map. Now, is there somewhere where you can wait till I get down to you?"

"I don't know." Then she said, "You can't come *here*."

"What . . . ? Listen, I *can* and I'm *coming*. Okay? It'll take me less than an hour. Now, is there somewhere you can *wait* for me?"

"Yes," said Jane.

"Are you sure?"

"Yes."

"Fine. Then listen. Listen, please, Jane. I'll be at the telephone box in one hour at the most. By half past three. Have you got that?"

"Yes."

"Good. Now, just . . . just wait for me. All right? I'll be as quick as I can. All right?"

"Yes," said Jane.

She continued to listen, but the voice had gone. Then, slowly, the shivering, too, began to subside, began to trickle

143

out of her, until, in the new stillness of the kiosk, there was only the hum of the telephone receiver left.

Jane lowered it to the limit of its plastic-covered cord, an inch or so from the floor, where it swung and twisted for a moment before succumbing to the inertia of its weight.

She straightened up. The humming continued, but farther away now, like a sound arising from the afternoon itself.

Jane pressed against the door of the kiosk, which eased open. She stepped out from the kiosk and stood upon the summit of the triangular grass mound, her hands held away from her body as though for balance. She looked, first right along the road, then left. Nothing was coming. With small, precise displacements of the feet, she turned around on the spot where she was standing and saw that the tree-tunneled lane that formed the third arm of the road junction was also empty. She turned back again. She descended the slope of the mound, crossed the main road and, reaching its other side, knelt, then lay down, among grass, dandelions and the fluted green branches of cow parsley.

Through a crisscross weave of stems and blades and pollen-heavy heads, she saw the sky slip past. Wind ruffled her skin. Insects climbed and descended her. The March afternoon cradled her between waking and sleeping, rocked her with the lullabye of its strong, invisible growth.

It wasn't until she heard the car draw up, the door slam, the footsteps clack across the road, that she slept.

144

Part 5

18

Then only for a moment. At once, Gary was shaking her, lifting her up from the ground and calling her name. His fingertips dug into her upper arm.

"Jane. Wake up."

She tried to resist. Eyes clenched, she thrust herself, immersed herself in the rediscovered heat and smell and strength of him. She muffled her ears in the softness of his leather jacket. With greedy nostrils, she sucked his smell of cheroot smoke.

"Jane. Come on. Wake up."

"No," she said. "Please."

"Come on."

He pushed her face away from his chest. She could taste the salt on the palm of his hand, feel the heat of his breath as it came and went on her eyelids.

"Jane, open your eyes. What have you done? You haven't taken anything, have you? Pills?"

"No," she said, hearing the tautness of his anger, yet

caring for nothing but the fact that he was there. She'd called and he had come. All the way from London, from his home and Henrietta, he had come.

"Then open your eyes. Look at me. Jane, if you don't look at me, I'm driving right back again."

"No!"

"All right then . . ."

"No!"

Her eyes sprang open.

She saw him: his brown hair standing up in tufts from the drive in the open car, his fine brows clenched, his lips parted, showing glistening, even, white teeth. He looked exactly as she'd known he would, standing there before her, his legs straddled for balance, his hands spread behind her shoulder blades, supporting her slumped weight.

But still Jane wished that he hadn't made her open her eyes, because now she was forced to see how incongruous it was that he was there, his London presence too sharp, too streamlined for the gentle country lane, his sports car parked at an embarrassed and temporary angle against the verge. Gary didn't belong here. He'd come, but he wouldn't stay.

Why hadn't she thought of that?

What *had* she thought?

"Gary."

"Yes, it's all right, I'm here. Now, do you think you can stand if I stop holding you?"

"Okay."

She allowed him to release her, fought the desire to cling to him still tighter.

"And you're sure you haven't taken any pills or anything?"

148

"Yes. I'm sure."

"Right."

He stepped back from her, ran the palms of his hands down his jeans.

"Now," he said. "First, what about at the school? Will they be missing you yet?"

"I don't know. I don't think so. What time is it?"

"Half past three. Twenty-five to four."

"I don't know. Maybe. They'll've finished games by now. I told . . . I said I wasn't feeling very well. They might think I'm still resting."

Jane felt the shivering begin again inside her, small, slow, but unmistakable.

"All right," said Gary. "Well, let's get somewhere less conspicuous, shall we? I know this isn't exactly Piccadilly Circus, but still. . . . Did you have anything with you?"

"No," said Jane.

"Right."

Gary stretched out a hand and laced its fingers through the fingers of one of Jane's. He led her across the road to where his car was parked. He released her hand. He opened the passenger door.

"In you hop," he said.

He circled the hood and climbed in beside her. He ignited the engine. Clicking shut his safety belt, he indicated the narrow, tree-tunneled lane that was the third arm of the junction and asked, "Where does that go?"

"Nowhere. Just past a few houses, then it dwindles out. We sometimes walk there."

"Good."

149

After that, he said nothing. Only the car spoke, as they swung into the mottled darkness of the lane, down a short incline, then up between high banks of tree roots and leaf mold.

Three minutes later, they reached the lane's summit. There, there was only a semicircle of gravel for cars and tractors to turn, an empty litter bin, a rusting hubcap and, beyond these, the woods.

Gary parked on the gravel beside the litter bin. He extinguished the car's engine. He unfastened his belt, climbed out of the car and walked into the woods. By the time that Jane had caught up with him, he was sitting on a fallen tree trunk and lighting a cheroot.

After the roar and screech of the drive, the silence in the clearing was intense; the stillness, also, with the wind held at bay by the encircling trees and the light dropping in solid shafts through gaps in the overhead branches.

Gary squeezed his lighter into the back pocket of his jeans. He raised the cheroot to his lips, drew on it, then released its smoke in a curling ribbon of white.

"Come and sit down," he said, when the ribbon had floated from sight.

Jane sat on the log, a foot or so from him, looked at her legs, at her heavy, brown shoes, at the carpet of twigs and last year's curled, dead leaves.

"How are you feeling?" asked Gary. "Calmer? A little bit calmer? All right. Now, tell me what on earth's happened."

"What I told you would," said Jane, still watching her feet.

"You mean, you've had a row with Audrey. Is that what you mean? She's still cross with you, about last weekend."

"Not just a row," said Jane. "A fight. She hit me, if you want to know. Look."

Unbuttoning her left shirt sleeve, rolling it back to reveal the raw, blood-pricked swelling, the surrounding bruise, she knew that it wasn't this that she wanted to say. But she heard his reaction, the jolt in his breathing, and was glad for that, at least.

"You see," she said.

"I don't . . ."

"She hit me. Hit me in the face, actually. I fell against a locker handle. That's how I did this."

"But *why?*"

"I *told* you. I *told* you she'd be furious."

"But you must've . . ."

"What?"

"Look, sweetheart, I just don't believe that Audrey sent you flying for no other reason than that you *argued* last weekend. That sort of anger doesn't last so long. It . . . You must have provoked her. You *know* you must have."

"Well," said Jane, standing up, feeling the trembling pulse through her again, like power. "Well, that just *shows* how damn little you understand. You don't even *begin* to . . . You don't . . . Don't you realize? We were best friends. And now, just because of you, she won't even *talk* to me."

"Not because of me," said Gary, standing too.

"Yes. Because you made me go out with you."

"Miss Rackham, we've discussed this, remember? Don't you remember agreeing how pointless it was, blaming other people when things appear to go wrong?"

"*You* may've agreed."

151

She was shouting now, shaking, poking the air with her fists.

"It's all right for *you*. You don't know what it's like in that place. Everybody hating me. Everybody staring at me, whispering about me behind my back. . . ."

She could see that he didn't believe her, knew how right he was not to, but could think of no other way of explaining the fear that she'd felt, the aloneness, the rejection, since returning to school the previous Sunday evening. By whatever means, she must make him understand that, must make him see how badly she needed his help.

"It's awful," she said. "Horrible. I loathe it. I loathe the lot of them. If you won't . . . I'm not going back there. I'm telling you, I'm not going back. I can't."

"What? Miss Rackham, you don't mean to tell me you're running away from school?"

"Not running away. That's stupid. That's . . . I'm leaving, that's all. Just not going back. Ever."

"I don't see a great deal of difference," said Gary, pressing his cheroot beneath one foot, stepping towards Jane and taking her fists in his hands. "But we'll call it 'leaving' if you prefer. Only, whichever way, you must see that, if you're in such a hurry to get away, it's because you don't really want to find out what it is that's gone wrong."

"I *know* what's gone wrong," said Jane, no longer shouting.

"Oh? What, then, Miss Rackham?"

"The whole thing. The whole place. They're *all* vile and stupid and . . . God, you don't *know*. You've no *idea* what they're like."

"No, I haven't, I agree. But how come *you*'ve suddenly

152

noticed? That's the point. You weren't talking like this at dinner on Saturday evening. You were laughing at the school, then. Joking about it with Audrey. And really quite fond of it, I suspect. So it must be *you* that's changed, or changing, mustn't it? Logically, Miss Rackham? And, if that's the case, then there's no point leaving the *school*."

"You're always . . ."

"What?"

"Why can't you just believe me? Why do you always say everything must be *my* fault?"

"Because it *is*. Just as everything that happens to me is my fault. Short of earthquakes, I suppose, or floods. But don't you see the power that that gives you? To change things? To make things the way that you want? Look, look, I'm willing to bet you all I've got. . . . No, all right, I do see that's not very tempting, but I'm willing to bet you *anything* that you could have made it up with Audrey quite easily by now, if you'd really tried. . . ."

"I couldn't."

"How do you know? Did you try?"

Jane hunched her shoulders. She turned her face to one side, saw a squirrel skedaddle up the trunk of a beech tree, pause, flick its tail, then spring into the upper branches. Her shivering had gone, to be replaced by a still fierce hatred, a fury against Gary for talking, joking, when she had cried to him for *help*.

"You didn't try, did you?" he said, one hand releasing its hold on her fists and rising to touch her face. "Oh, please, sweetheart, don't *scowl* so. I know you think I'm being horrible, but, don't you see, it's because I respect you too much to humor you. You're an intelligent, caring, adult

153

person, beneath all the screaming and shouting, and, you know, it's only because you won't *admit* to that that you're feeling so very uncomfortable. Why don't you *go* back to Audrey, *tell* her you want to be friends again. It's not easy, I know, but honestly, sweetheart, you're capable of it. And it's got to be better than the panic and unhappiness you're feeling at the moment, hasn't it?"

"No!" said Jane. "No, I *can't* go back. Gary, please, you've got to help me. You said you would. You said if I rang . . ."

Then, with a sudden, strong certainty, Jane remembered something: the fluorescent-lit kitchen of the Crofts' flat and Gary holding her, Gary rocking her, Gary's lips moving gently against her hair. With a judder of relief, her body began to cry.

"Oh, please Jane, no, don't go and make it hard for us both."

"I'm *not*. It's not *me*."

She swung away from him, sure that his hand around her wrists would whip her back.

"Please, Jane," he said. "Don't cry. Jane, don't, it won't help."

But he was holding her against him now, was stroking her head, was rocking her, the way that he had before. And it was easy for Jane to search out his lips, to find them and press them open beneath her own.

"I love you, Gary."

"Jane, sweetheart, you don't."

But his arms continued to grasp her waist, his mouth to travel her face, her neck, her ears. She could feel his hot breath over her skin, the crashing of his heart against her sweater.

Then,

"Damn you!"

And his arms were no longer around her, were rigid between them, like bars to hold her at bay.

"God, I could . . ."

His teeth glistened. His nostril wings trembled. The stubble on his upper lip was beaded with sweat.

"What *is* it?" said Jane. "Gary, it's all right, I *love* you."

"Shut up! Shut up, you bloody idiot. You don't know what the hell you're talking about."

"I do. Please, you've got to believe me."

"Shut up, did you hear me?"

"Please, Gary, you can't leave me. You've got to take me with you."

"Like hell I . . . Look, look, just . . ."

His eyes scanned the trees and bushes around them, as though they were desperate for help.

Jane said, "I don't understand. Tell me, what did I do wrong?"

"Nothing. It's me. It's my fault. Look, please, can we just go back to the car?"

"But Gary, didn't you hear what I said? I love you."

"Yes, I heard. . . ." He paused, the fear beginning to drain away from his features. Then, more softly, he said, "Of course I heard. But Jane, it just isn't true."

"You can't *know*."

"Look, can we go back to the car? It's about to rain, anyway. Feel. Shall we go?"

With a nod of his head, he indicated the direction of their return journey.

Then he half smiled.

"Come on," he said. "It really is about to piss down. Can't you hear it? Can't you hear the rain, crackling up in the treetops?"

"I don't care about that."

"Well, *I* do. Come on."

He turned and began to walk away from her, towards the lay-by. The undergrowth made agitated noises. The treetops waved. The darkening air hummed with needlepoint spittles of rain.

Standing where Gary had left her, Jane drew into her lungs enough breath to shatter, with his name, all the sounds of the woods; then, in silence, released it and set off after him through the trees.

19

By the time that they'd emerged from the woods into the comparative light of the open, rain was sweeping in hard, unbroken, diagonal lines.

"Hurry," said Gary, fumbling with the fastenings that held open the car's canvas roof. "Get in. You're getting soaked."

Jane walked to the driver's door and opened it. She sat down on the damp leather seat. Her hair, drenched in the few seconds that it had taken to cross the gravel lay-by, stuck to her head and dripped its surplus water down her neck. Her hands were pink, wet and cold.

Having drawn the roof up over Jane and fixed it into place, Gary opened the passenger door and climbed into the car beside her.

"So, here we are again," he said. "We seem to spend most of our time sheltering in here from the rain, don't we? You soaked right through?"

"No."

"It certainly came down, didn't it?" he said. "Well now . . ."

He looked at his watch. Jane saw him look at the damp-misted face of his watch, then back at her, his mouth smiling, his green eyes watchful and still.

"Quarter past four," he said. "What do you think? Are they likely to have missed you yet?"

"I'm not going back there," said Jane.

The smile still shaping his mouth, Gary said, "You know you've got to."

"I'm going with you," said Jane.

"And you know *that*'s impossible."

Their eyes held one another's, Jane's as steady as Gary's. Outside the car, water gurgled across the gravel in rivulets and eddied where it was dammed by tarmac road. No birds sang. The only sounds were of rain and earth and battered vegetation.

Gary said, "Besides, it wouldn't help. It wouldn't solve anything."

"You think you know it all, don't you?" said Jane, removing her eyes from his and running the tip of her index finger around the steering wheel's plastic rim. "What's good for me, what's bad for me, what I'm feeling, *why* I'm feeling it. You keep telling me I'm not a baby, but you go on *treating* me as though I am one, don't you? I've told you I love you. Why won't you believe me? Do you think I'm too *young* to love?"

"No, Miss Rackham, not too young. But . . ."

"What, then?"

"Just . . . too selfish. You're not even capable of friendship yet. The *giving* that it involves. And, until you are, you won't be capable of love."

"Oh, thanks! So you don't even care that your damn sister-in-law *hit* me."

"We're not talking about Audrey. We're talking about you."

"Well, let's stop then, shall we?"

Jane gripped the steering wheel and twisted it as far around as the parked tires would let her. She leaned her weight against the wheel. She stared at the floor, at the car's pedals: the clutch and the brake pedals with their ridged rubber casings, the worn metal accelerator.

"Okay," said Gary.

"Good," said Jane.

She released the steering wheel. She raised her eyes to the steamy window beside her, saw the rain continue to rush across the gravel of the lay-by, glug in deep channels, pound against the body of the car: a dead, pointless wetness, aimed at no one and nothing in particular, mindless of where, or when, or upon whom it fell. Before she was born, the rain must have fallen like this, must always have fallen like this; nor, without her, would it behave any differently. Neither rain, trees, road, car, nor anything would be affected in the smallest degree were she no longer there to watch them.

Her throat ached, as though a cord were being tightened around it. Her eyes pricked, but she was damned if she was going to cry.

She heard Gary move.

She said, "I can drive us. I've driven my father's car, before, at home, in the ponies' field. I bet this one's just as easy."

"Easier, probably. Jane, please, there's no need to be so angry. Maybe . . . Maybe I shouldn't have come. It's as much my fault as yours. More, really, because I knew that I couldn't help you. You're the only one who can do that. But . . . Oh, I don't know, sweetheart. You're so very unhappy and . . . What about your parents? You never talk about your parents. Are you close to them? Can you write to them?"

"Oh, of course I can *write*. I don't suppose they have time to read my letters, but I can write."

"Why do you say that?"

"Because it's true. My mother spends her whole time having babies and my father spends his whole time being witty. He's a television critic. Mrs. Croft thinks he's the best thing in the Sunday papers. Look, let me have the keys."

"Are you the oldest?"

"What? Yes. God, there's been so many since me, they've probably forgotten I exist. Go on, give me the keys."

"You think they don't love you anymore. Is that it?"

"Don't be so . . . Don't be so bloody stupid. Of course they do. Of course they *love* me. Look . . ."

"All right."

Gary dug into the pocket of his jacket and produced the leather-tabbed ring on which he kept his car keys.

"You can start her. It's the key with the square head. But, Jane, you must understand that the sort of attention the younger ones need, your younger sisters or brothers or whatever they are . . ."

"I don't want to *talk* about it. Okay?"

Steadying her right hand, Jane eased the key into the ignition lock. She checked the gears, wriggling the stick to ensure that they were in neutral. She touched the hand brake. She moved her bottom around in the seat and stretched her legs to see whether she could reach the control pedals.

She said, "I'll have to have the seat closer."

"There's a lever down to your right, by the floor. Look, sweetheart, you wouldn't *really* want to be two again or six or ten, would you? Not allowed to do this. Not allowed to do that. Everything arranged for you. . . ."

"*Where*'s the lever?"

"On the door side."

"Oh, yes."

She depressed the lever and shuffled the driver's seat closer to the pedals, the steering wheel, the dashboard. She made sure that the seat was locked in its new position. She leaned forward and, with her left hand, turned the ignition key.

"Pump a bit on the accelerator," said Gary.

"I know how to do it. It's just slightly different, that's all. Where's the windscreen wiper? The knob for the windscreen wiper, which one is it?"

"Wait till you've got the engine started first."

"Just show me which one it *is*."

Gary showed her.

She switched it down, then up again. The curtain of water that her action had swept from the wide glass screen was at once replaced. Then, pumping with her right foot on the accelerator pedal, she once more turned the ignition key and kept it in a horizontal position against the kick of its sprung resistance.

"Damn. What's the matter with this thing? Why won't it start? I can always do it," she said.

Gary leaned towards her as though to help her, then, abruptly, withdrew. Jane heard him sit back in his seat.

Her throat tightened harder, but she tried again and, this time, although nothing that she had done was different from before, the engine caught. The key sprang back. A loud and violent roaring sound, a sound whose volume, whose very existence, depended upon the whim of her foot, filled the car with its power.

"It's going," she said.

"So I hear," said Gary, his voice quiet, detached from the engine's excitement, as though he were somewhere else.

Forcing herself not to look at him, Jane said, "I'm going to drive it."

"Very well."

"Don't you think I can?"

"I'll see, shan't I?"

With the engine held at roaring pitch, Jane turned the steering wheel, depressed the clutch, moved the gear stick into first and lowered the hand brake to the floor. Her mouth was dry. She breathed in short, absentminded gasps. The awakened power of the car strained beneath her feet and struggled against the palms of her hands, but she couldn't relinquish it, not now, not unless she were *forced* to. It was hers. She'd taken it and, to whatever end, she had no choice but to use it.

She started the windscreen wipers again. Pulling on the steering wheel, she twisted the tires farther around against the gravel. Then, slowly, carefully, thighs aching with caution, she played the accelerator against the clutch and the car began to move forward.

She held the steering wheel at the extremity of its lock. The car's hood inched around to face the road.

"What now?" said Gary.

"What?"

"What are you going to do now?"

"I'm driving. On the road. Why not?"

Maintaining a slow forward momentum with the accelerator pedal, she allowed the steering wheel to spin back counterclockwise through her fingers. The car veered a few inches to the left. She rectified the error, then, no longer circling, but moving straight ahead, crossed the humped boundary between lay-by and solid tarmac road.

Gear stick shifted into second, speedometer needle rising to fifteen miles per hour, high, tree-trunked banks whipping past her on either side, Jane was driving a real car on a real road.

"I haven't got a license, but what does that matter?" she said.

"You tell me," said Gary.

Neither anger, nor criticism, nor emotion of any kind crossed the gap between them with his words. Jane put more weight onto her right foot and moved the gears into third.

The road banks began to swerve in on her, first from the

right, then from the left. Between the sweeps of the wind-screen wipers, a fine spray misted her vision before being swept once more to safety by the return of the thin metal arms. As the speedometer needle touched twenty, Jane released her foot from the accelerator, but the downward impulsion of the hill sucked the car onward. She braked; not completely, but enough to negotiate the bends and to reduce the transmission to second for the T junction at the bottom of the hill. Then, on the wider, flatter, straighter road, she accelerated again.

"Okay, Jane, if you're going to go on with this, you're at least going to put your seat belt on."

As he spoke, Gary changed his position beside her, but the movement was smooth, unflustered, and the voice was careless still. The engine's roar had more emotion than Gary's voice, the hiss of the tires more anger.

"Come on, the seat belt," said Gary.

"What's the matter?" asked Jane. "Are you frightened?"

"Yes. In fact . . ."

He wasn't frightened. If he were frightened, he'd be shouting at her, he'd be wrenching the wheel from her hands.

A grocer's van nosed out through a gateway beside the road and swung its tall, gray body towards them. Jane plunged her right foot to the floor. She held her breath, as the car slipped between the van's sway and the hawthorn hedge to her left.

"There's nothing to be frightened of. Look, I did that perfectly."

"All right. That's enough. We've had enough now. Stop, Jane. Draw up here."

"No, I'm enjoying it."

"It's my car, Jane, and I'm telling you to stop. Look, sweetheart, it's not just you and me. There's other people on this road."

"That's *their* bad luck."

Eliston's Woods had materialized to their left: the beech trees and the oak trees, the saplings, the brambles and the ferny undergrowth blurred into a cohesive, pale-green band, behind rain and speed.

"You wanted me to go back to school, didn't you? Well, that's where I'm going," she said.

"Just, not so fast."

"This isn't *fast*."

"It is, for someone who's never driven properly before. And it's raining, Jane. Slow down!"

That was better. His voice had tightened its pitch. He'd shouted and his right hand had shot out to touch hers on the steering wheel.

"Go on, stop me then," said Jane.

He withdrew his hand.

"How *can* I, you bloody idiot?"

"Why not, if you're so frightened?"

She accelerated. The speedometer needle hit forty-five miles per hour. The steering wheel hummed in her hands and the tires sang high above the engine.

"Go on," she said. "Stop me, if you want to."

"What the hell do you expect me to do? Knock you unconscious? Drag you out of your seat?"

"What?"

"I *can't* stop you, girl."

He was right.

As the rain continued to smash against the windscreen, to leap from the windscreen wipers' blades, as Eliston's Woods continued to charge towards them before slicing away to their left, as the tops of the white school gateposts, like mayflowers, at first, then more solid, rushed closer and closer, Jane knew that Gary was right. Unless he wanted her to overturn the car, there was nothing that he could do to make her stop. She had rendered his strength impotent. She, only, was in control.

Yet what could *she* do? Decelerate? Change down, through third, to second gear? In a world reduced to walking pace and the splash of falling rain, draw over to the side of the road and submissively park?

And then what?

By now, not only the tops of the school gateposts, but their whole white-painted height, was visible; also the dark opening on whose either side, like bored and inattentive guards, they stood. Thirty yards away from these, Jane tensed the toes of her right foot to withdraw from the accelerator a small amount of pressure, then, teeth clenched, face tight, she paddled her hands around to five o'clock on the steering wheel, swung them, together, up and counterclockwise and, at the height of the turn into the school drive, released the weight of her foot back onto the floor of the car.

There was a moment when they were moving on two wheels. Pebbles spurted against the glass of Gary's window. Something screeched. Something burned.

But the raised tires bounced back, dislodging with the

violence of their fall the grip of one of Jane's hands, and, having plowed a short slalom from side to side of the drive, righted themselves with scarcely a loss of speed.

"For Christ's sake. Jane. For God's sake. Stop it. What're you trying to do? Do you know where you are? The school's just around . . ."

"I know. Isn't that where you wanted me? Well, that's where we're going. That's *just* where we're going."

"Jane, please, I . . . Jane. Look out. Jane!"

One moment, it hadn't been there. One moment, there'd been nothing but the muddy onrush of fields and drive and sky.

The next, it was as clear and detailed as a color photograph stuck to the windscreen, with tape, for Jane to study: a pair of wide, yellow eyes with vertical slits for pupils; a mouth peeled open to reveal its pink interior, its hooked teeth, its hunched, pink tongue; a black nose; black fur; white fur, glistening with silver.

"Jane!"

She couldn't find the brake pedal.

"Jane!"

Her foot slipped off smooth metal and something hard smashed into the back of her ankle. She tried again. The car yelled, plowed on its axis, stopped.

Shaking, scraping her knuckles, bruising the tips of her fingers, she fumbled for the door handle.

"All right Jane, just wait a second. Wait a second. Are you okay? Have you hurt yourself?"

"Aziz," said Jane. "That was . . ."

"I know. But are *you* okay? First . . ."

The door swung open. Jane tumbled from the car. Her legs were like soft weights, like sacks of sand preventing her from moving.

"Az, Az . . ."

Nor would her voice obey her brain's shouting, but stuck, half-formed, in her throat. After the drunken inevitability of the drive, the all-conquering, all-annihilating speed of it, this quietness, this immobility was unacceptable. Jane couldn't believe in it.

"It isn't true," she tried to say. "It hasn't happened. It hasn't. It hasn't happened."

But the gray school drive remained unmoved in front of her, the tired rain fell softly, the tipped, bottle-green body of the car lay silent and still in its resting place, halfway up a bank.

Somewhere, not more than a hundred yards away, around a bend in the drive, girls would be settling down to their evening prep. Mrs. Bailey would be shaking open a library book to the page she'd turned down, as a mark, the night before. Miss Anthony would be in her drawing room, smiling at a mistake in a Civics essay, perhaps, reaching down, without looking, to stroke the head of the cat that had come to rub itself against her leg; the tortoiseshell-and-white she-cat; or the tabby Pythagoras; not knowing that Aziz was dead.

A minute ago, he'd been scampering across the drive from the shelter of one clump of bushes to another, rain spangling his coat, his small, black ears laid back, his tail horizontal and weaving for balance. Jane had seen him. Then Jane had killed him.

She felt Gary touch her elbows and turn her around to face him. She didn't protest.

"Are you hurt?" he asked. "Are you hurt *anywhere*?"

"No," she said.

"Thank God for that, anyway. Okay, now we'll go and see if we can find the cat."

"He's dead," she said, wondering how long it would be before she believed it, instead of just knowing it.

"He may not be. They're pretty astonishing, cats. I've known them to survive the most incredible things. Just get up and shake themselves and walk away. As if nothing had happened. Come on, sweetheart."

Jane looked at him. How could he tell such a lie?

Then she understood. It was because he was free from guilt. Innocent, he could afford to comfort both himself and her. But *she* wasn't free. She was guilty. Alone and forever, she was guilty.

"I can't *see* him," said Gary.

Jane looked at the rain-shining, empty curve of the drive.

She said, "He'll've gone off into the hedges to die. They do that."

"He may just be hurt. Come on. I'll . . ."

"No," said Jane. "I'll look for him. Please. You go. I'll look for him."

"You mustn't blame yourself, Jane. He just leaped out. I mean . . ."

Gary stopped.

Jane said, "Go on, go home."

Gary stepped back from the hedgerow into which he had been peering. He turned to look at her, standing a few yards from her. The air was thick with fine rain and dusk. He narrowed his green eyes.

"Go on," she said. "You'd better. There's nothing you can do."

"Was he the headmistress's?"

"Yes."

"I could come with you and talk to her . . ."

"How?" said Jane. "What'd you say? That you were just letting me have a little spin in your car and . . . No. Just go away. Please, Gary. This is *my* . . . This . . . *I*'ve got to sort this out. Haven't I? Haven't I?"

"I don't know," said Gary, touching his forehead with the thumb and middle finger of his left hand.

"Well, I do. Gary, please, go back to London. It must be . . . I don't know. What time is it? Won't Henrietta be worried about where you are or something?"

"No, that's all right. She won't be back from work yet. Look, Jane . . ."

"No, please, I mean it."

"I just wish I knew if you were *capable* of coping by yourself."

Jane shrugged. What difference did it make if she were capable, or not? She had no choice. She *must* cope.

"God, I wish . . ."

"Yes, but it's *happened*," she said, believing it at last.

She looked at Gary, saw his neat, hard body hunched beneath the drizzle, his short hair netted with rain, his drawn-in eyebrows, his clenched, green eyes. Beside what had happened, beside death, he seemed suddenly small and helpless, no stronger or abler than she. Remote, too, a long

169

way away, like someone she'd never known.

"Yes, *you*'ll cope," he said suddenly. "Maybe . . . Well, anyway . . ."

He turned to look at the car, then back.

" 'Bye, Gary," said Jane. "And . . ."

"Yes, I know. Well, good-bye, Miss Rackham."

"Good-bye."

Part 6

20

It was strange to watch the car being reversed down the bank, then shunted backwards and forwards, a couple of yards at a time, until it was once more facing in the direction from which it had come. So obedient and ordinary it seemed, not like a machine that had killed.

As it drew level with the place where Jane was standing, Gary leaned across its passenger seat and unwound the window. Eyes narrowed as though he were still protecting them from the rain, or as though he were thinking of something, trying to work something out, he looked at her. He parted his lips. He inhaled through stretched nostrils, then clamped his mouth shut, swept his eyes from Jane's face and, without reclosing the window, withdrew into the dimness of the car's interior and drove away.

When she could neither see him anymore nor hear him, when the vacuum of his going had been replenished by the drip of water from twigs and the dying, chill brown-gray of late afternoon, Jane clenched her fists and began to search the hedgerow. It was difficult to see anything among the twisted roots and stems that grew atop the bank beside the drive. A thick smell of leaf mold choked her nostrils, making it hard to breathe.

"Aziz," she whispered, from time to time. "Aziz," knowing that there could be no answer.

"Aziz. Please puss. Puss, puss, puss, puss. Aziz."

But the hedge was three or four feet thick in places and already it was hard to be sure exactly where along the drive it had happened, the accident. There were skid marks, gray, curving ribbons across the tarmac, but these had a calm, established look, as though they had been there always. They'd nothing to do with the thud that had sickened Jane's stomach, with the flying, black-and-white body, with the ripped, pink mouth.

Suddenly, crumpling onto the bank below the hedge, seeing, in the valley opposite, a line of munching sheep like wooden toys, seeing beyond the sheep how old and peaceful seemed Eliston's Woods, hearing the chapel clock begin to sound, Jane knew what was left for her to do.

This, what had happened out here on the drive, was over, irrevocably over. Let someone else find the body. Let someone else pick it up, hug it to them and cry the comforting tears of unguilty grief. To her, even that must be denied.

Six o'clock.

She forced her imagination inside the school. Six o'clock. Yes, all of the girls would be at prep and most of the staff would be supervising them. Those who weren't would either have gone home or be in the staff room. It didn't matter. The point was that they'd be out of the way, behind closed doors.

There was one person only with whom Jane would speak, with whom she *must* speak. Miss Anthony had to be told. She couldn't be allowed to go on expecting Aziz. Jane must tell her.

Then . . .

Then nothing.

She stood up from where she'd been kneeling. The reverberation of the clock's last stroke had died. She must hurry. In half an hour, in twenty-five minutes, the halls and stairs and corridors of the school would be filled with hurrying people: with maids preparing supper; with girls who'd stare at her, or stop to ask her questions, or express concern; with shouting matrons and under-matrons; with the duty-mistress; with the grating shrill of the Haggis.

She raised her eyes towards the bend in the drive. She began to walk.

21

"Come in," called the headmistress, her voice clipped and harsh even through the paneled wood of the drawing-room door.

"Come *in* I said."

Squeezing her eyes shut, trying to believe in the thing that was about to happen, seeing only darkness, Jane turned the handle and stepped inside the room.

"So. So, Jane Rackham. So, you've decided that it's at last convenient for you to come and see me, have you? At . . ."

Erect behind her mahogany writing table, the headmistress turned her wrist to look at the flat, round, silver watch that she wore.

"At twenty past six," she said. "You feel at liberty to interpret my requests that loosely, do you?"

Failing to understand what she was being asked, Jane stood where she was, waiting for a pause in the nonsense, waiting for silence.

"You did hear the announcement at teatime, I suppose? That you were to come and see me. Your friend Audrey didn't seem to find any difficulty in following my instructions."

Jane said, "Audrey?"

What was she talking about? What was Miss Anthony talking about? What had *Audrey* got to do with anything? She belonged in some past that no longer mattered; not here; not now.

She said, "But I wasn't *at* tea."

"Really?" said Miss Anthony. "I see. You don't take your *meals* when you're supposed to, now, either. Is that what I'm supposed to understand?" she asked. "Is it? Because I should tell you, Jane, that if I don't get a fairly convincing explanation for the awful deterioration in your behavior over the last week or so, I'm going to be forced to take the sort of action that I'm sure we'd both regret. Do you understand me?"

"Yes, Miss Anthony," said Jane.

But she didn't. How could the headmistress still believe that her behavior over the last week or so was relevant? Didn't she know, hadn't she even sensed, the intraversable distance by which Jane had removed herself from such

176

stupid misdemeanors as talking in prep, impersonating the staff and wearing sneakers, instead of boots, for lacrosse?

"And would you mind just showing me your hands a moment? I thought so. They're disgusting. They look as though you've been digging around in the mud. Well, you'll start by scrubbing your nails and putting a comb through your hair. You make me feel ill just to look at you. Go on. Go and see if you can't do something to yourself before supper. I'll see you after chapel."

"No, please," said Jane. "I mean, please, I've got to *tell* you something. Now."

"I *beg* your pardon. Didn't you hear what I said? I'll see you after *chapel.* Oh, now, listen to me, my dear girl, this is really getting beyond a joke. Your insolence isn't even redeemed by charm. Maybe *you* think, somewhere inside that twisted head of yours, that you're being witty, or interesting, but let me assure you that you are not. No, on the contrary, Jane, I'm afraid I find you . . . Yes? Come in!"

Another knock had sounded on the drawing-room door.

With both hands, Jane gripped her forehead, as the door opened, as the voice of the school secretary said, "Oh, I'm sorry, Miss Anthony. I didn't realize you'd got someone with you."

"That's quite all right, Mary. Jane Rackham's just leaving."

"No . . ." began Jane and, at that moment, a movement disengaged itself from one of the sagging armchairs and slithered with a thud to the floor.

Jane's breathing stopped.

The tortoiseshell-and-white she-cat stretched, tipped back her head and opened her mouth in a yawn.

Jane's breathing resumed, but faster and more shallow than before. Her pulse beat triple-pace within her stomach.

"*What* did you say, Jane?"

She had to interrupt, this *moment*. Before the cat could finish stretching and come to rub against her leg, before Miss Anthony could waste, in irritation and dislike, the emotions that she would need for her fury and hatred, she *had* to speak.

"Jane, I told you to *go*."

"What?"

She had to stop her. She couldn't let the headmistress go on exposing herself to the indignity of being winded in full spate. Yet, how could she tell her with the secretary in the room? How, while the secretary tipped her pink face to one side and twisted her mouth at one corner in a private, self-satisfied smile, could Jane say, "Miss Anthony, Aziz is dead"?

She looked from the secretary to the headmistress. She tried to open her mouth.

"Jane, are you *deliberately* being insolent? Are you *deliberately* not listening to a word I'm saying?"

"I'm sorry," said Jane, "but . . ."

She couldn't remember the secretary's surname. Robins? Robinson? No, Miss Robinson had been the one before.

She said, "Please, Miss Anthony, please couldn't I talk to you alone?"

"Couldn't you what?" said the headmistress. "I'm not sure I heard you properly. No, Mary, stay where you are. We've yet to reach the situation where you take your orders from a *girl*. Even from one as arrogant and insolent and rude as Jane Rackham, I'm glad to say.

You'll apologize to Miss Clark *at once*, Jane."

"I'm sorry, Miss Clark. I'm sorry, but, Miss Anthony, please, this really is private."

"Oh, there's nothing in the slightest *bit* private about your behavior, my dear."

"No, it's not . . ."

"Will you *stop* interrupting? There's nothing private about it at all. I wish there were. I do wish there were. But I've been hearing about it, from every corner, day in, day out, until I am just about sick of it. Do you hear me? You're difficult, you're rude, you behaved like a *tart* on the train going up to London last weekend. . . ."

By now, the headmistress was crouched across the writing table, her hands spread out to grip its either edge. Her wrists, protruding from the crisp, double-buttoned cuffs of her blouse, flexed and unflexed, flexed and unflexed, as though she were testing their strength.

"Tell me," she said. "I'd like to know. Do you seriously imagine that by daubing your face with powder and grease and great black smudges you make yourself look attractive? Do you? Is that what you think? Because I saw what you did to yourself for the school dance last summer, my dear. I didn't say anything at the time. I didn't want to embarrass you. But, honestly, you looked ridiculous. Several people remarked on it."

Jane stared at the headmistress, stared so hard that she was no longer focusing on any one feature, but absorbing the whole, hunched shape. Her eyes felt powerless, hypnotized by the ring of artificial light in which Miss Anthony crouched, her malice throbbing through the room like pus. Jane could hear the remorseless beat of its poison.

179

Against her right foot, the tortoiseshell-and-white she-cat had bent to rub her small, demanding head and she tried to concentrate on this, tried to remember the sentence she had come to speak: "Aziz is dead."

"I'm telling you this for your own good, Jane. You've been allowed to get away with thinking you were special for too long. And you're not, you know. Your intelligence is scarcely more than average, whatever the other girls may like to think. No, your head's been rather swollen over the last few years, I'm afraid. I don't know why. None of the work you've ever done for *me* has been more than passable. In fact, your last essay was so substandard that I've had to fail you on it. C minus, I think, though it was hardly worth that. Or do you think it was worth more? Do *you*, maybe, think it *wasn't* a messy, misspelled, shallow piece of scrawl, hardly worthy of a first-former?"

"I don't know," said Jane, aware, not so much of the question, as of the pause, of the sign that she'd at last been given an opportunity to speak.

She said, "I must tell you something, Miss Anthony."

She felt dizzy. The room, the light, the woman's looming figure, the insistent pressure of the cat's head against her calf, all seemed to be shrinking away from her. Her lips had become thick. Her tongue had swollen to fill her mouth.

"Oh yes?" She heard the headmistress say. "This is fascinating. *What* must you tell me?"

What?

Jane *knew* what.

"I've killed Aziz. Aziz is dead. I killed him."

The words sounded clear and articulate inside her head. But she couldn't produce them, not while the air still stank of Miss Anthony's sarcasm, not while Miss Anthony's strength lay back debauched. How could she? It wouldn't be fit. Taken off her guard, the headmistress would flounder in petty, undignified emotions, would drag Aziz's death down to a level it didn't deserve, would, worst of all, more unbearable than all, be powerless to inflict upon Jane the punishment that she needed.

She should've spoken sooner. However hard it had seemed then, she should've known that it would get no easier.

Why, why hadn't Miss Anthony let her? Couldn't she see, for heaven's sake, couldn't she *hear* the horror inside Jane? It was *her* horror too, wasn't it? Was she so deaf, so blind, so devoid of understanding?

"I'm waiting. Miss Clark and I are on tenterhooks to hear this new revelation."

On a spasm of anger, Jane almost told her then, but the impulse died before it was fully born and she turned the half-formed gesture into a shrug.

"No, you don't surprise me," said Miss Anthony. "What was it? You thought you'd found some brilliant excuse, then realized it wasn't so clever after all? You bore me, Jane, I'm afraid. You're not only rude and disobedient and quite ordinary as a scholar, but you're so full of your own importance that you haven't even the grace to accept criticism. Go on. Leave my room, will you? And go straight to your dormitory. You can find out from Audrey, tomorrow, what I've set you to do, for your behavior on the train last Saturday. Other than that, I don't see any point in talking to you further. I just don't want to hear *from* you, or *about* you again. Do you understand?"

"Yes," said Jane.

Loathing for the headmistress filled her, excluding in its totality even *self*-loathing; excluding even love for Aziz.

"Go on, then. To your dormitory."

Miss Anthony had got up from her chair behind the writing table. The secretary had moved to one of the filing cabinets, was pulling open a deep, paper-stuffed drawer.

The headmistress said, "Go on. I'd rather not see your face one second longer."

"Good night, Miss Anthony," said Jane. "Good night, Miss Clark."

As she left the drawing room, the bell for the end of prep began to ring.

22

She passed the prefect with the handbell in the entrance hall.

"Jane Rackham! Why aren't you in prep? It's only just time to stop."

She didn't answer.

"I'm going to report you!"

She left the hall and turned up the wooden pupils' staircase. She climbed the stairs two and three at a time, but not hurrying. At the first-floor landing, she encountered a stream of middle-formers newly released from their classroom. These noticed her, took care to make themselves small as she passed among them, but continued talking as though she weren't there, with voices loud from having so long been silent.

At the second floor, Jane disengaged herself from their swirling, bubbling flow and walked alone along the corridor to the loo.

Inside, she bolted the door behind her. She stayed where she was, not sitting down, her eyesight turned inwards upon the calm and undemanding blankness of her hatred for Miss Anthony.

After a moment, a fresh surge of voices and clattering footsteps burst up the stairs and along the passage. Someone shook the handle of the loo door.

"Who's in there? Hurry up. I'm bursting."

It was Miranda Spurling. The closeness of the voice, the intimacy of it, surprised Jane, but didn't frighten her. She knew that she was safe. She didn't even attempt to hold her breath.

"Come on. Hurry up. I'm going to wet my pants in a second."

"Who's in zere?"

That was Simone de Preville.

"I don't know. Ruth, probably. Come on, Bummly, put that book away. There's people out here waiting."

"I'm going down ze ozzer end."

"Me too. Wait for me. Hey, let me go first, will you, Prevy? I'm hopping."

During the next half an hour, there were a dozen attempts on the loo door, a dozen jigglings of its handle, a dozen angry, urgent requests. Jane listened to them all, but was neither moved nor worried. Her hatred against Miss Anthony had become a world unto itself, sustaining her and making her inviolate.

At seven o'clock, the bell for supper rang. Like a bath

from which the plug has been removed, the corridor emptied. Voices and footsteps spiraled away down the drain of the stairwell, grew faint, then disappeared in a vortex of spinning silence.

Jane waited. When the silence had stopped spinning, had become still, she slid the iron bolt from its clasp and walked back along the corridor.

Within her empty dormitory, she undressed. She shook, smoothed out and folded each article of her clothing, before laying it across the seat of her bedside chair. She folded her bedspread before hanging it over the rail at the foot of her bed. Peeling back the blankets and the top sheet, she exposed a neat, equilateral triangle of white. Then she crossed to the door. She switched the lights off. She returned to her bed, climbed into it and tucked the sheet and blanket tight about her.

Lying with her face towards the ceiling, her throat swollen and closed, her face hot, her mind empty of everything but her hatred for the headmistress, she allowed her eyes to close. Pitch-blackness settled like soot behind the lids.

She slept.

23

"Hey, Plain Face, wake up. Wake up. The bell's gone."

"No," she said.

Not another. Hadn't there been enough? Bright, copper handbells with polished, wooden handles; gigantic, black-mouthed church bells swinging from their stocks; a bell in the shape of a shepherdess, sharp and tinkling; metal tongues clonging in metal cups; all through the night, no matter how Jane'd twisted her head from side to side, the bells had chased her. Like bees, they'd swarmed around her with their wild, mad singing, each voice on a different note and in a different tone, but all commanding, imperious, inescapable.

She'd run. She'd tried to tear her head from her body, to throw it away, knowing that it was her head that the bells were after.

She'd fallen, rolled down a long, bumpy hillside, the strands of mown grass that bestrewed the hill wrapping themselves about her in a cocoon. But even through this protective covering, she'd heard them. Even when most of the bells had tired, there'd been one that had carried on: a soft, low note, repeated only after its preceding echo had died, so faint, sometimes, that Jane thought it must, at last, have worn itself out. But it never did, just rang on and on and on and on in the darkness.

"Plain!"

"No," she said. "Not another. Please, leave me alone."

"What's the matter? For goodness' sake, what're you talking about? The *bell*'s rung. Didn't you hear it? You're not ill or something, are you?"

Jane opened her eyes.

Rose Mercer, shirt hanging loose and unbuttoned, a pair of tights bunched like a dishcloth in one hand, stared down at her.

"Are you ill?" asked Rose. "Is that why you went to bed early? The Haggis said you'd got your period. Is that what it is?"

"What?" said Jane.

She looked past Rose; saw Loretta, who gave a quick nod of her large, blonde, open-mouthed head, then bent to fasten a shoe; saw Ruth Bottomly struggling with the waistband of her skirt.

She pushed back the covers.

"Hell, how long've I got?" she asked, sliding from her bed to the floor.

"Don't worry. You've got time," said Ruth.

"Well, *I*'d hurry," said Rose, "if I were you."

Jane pulled off her pajamas.

"What? Five minutes?" she said.

"Yes," said Ruth.

"Just," said Rose.

Loretta said, "We thought you *must*'ve heard it. We thought you were just being stupid. You know, you were whispering things to yourself and trying to put your head underneath the pillow. We just thought you were pretending or something."

Jane poured cold water from a jug into her washbowl. She lowered her face beneath the water's surface, shook it once, twice, then, with a gasp, withdrew it. She groped for her towel. She dried her face. She took the toothbrush from her mug and covered its bristles with paste.

"Wednesday," she said. "Urgh. Bacon and tinned tomatoes."

"You don't sound ill to *me*," said Rose. "Are you *sure* you had your period yesterday?"

"What?" said Jane, through the white foam in her mouth.

"You know," said Rose.

186

One of the jollier under-matrons swung the top half of her body around the dormitory door and called, "Hurry up, now. Get a move on. Chapel in three minutes."

Jane spat into her washbowl.

She said, "*Three* minutes."

"Do you think you're going to make it?" asked Rose, gloatingly pessimistic.

More and more people were moving along the corridor now. Doors slammed open and shut as though a train were about to leave a station. Within the dormitory, everybody but Jane had finished dressing.

"Well, go on," she said. "What're you all waiting for?"

No one *ever* waited for anyone else. They leaped out of bed, they washed, they put on their clothes and then, as fast as was possible without breaking into a run, hurried down through the school and out across the courtyard to the foot of the chapel stairs. There, a frowning prefect slowed them down, hissed, "Okay, you lot, one at a time now. Don't push. I said, *don't push.* You! Come and stand here. Do you think you're queuing for the cinema or something?"

It'd be Valerie Creighton this morning. It was usually her, on a Wednesday, Jane remembered.

"Go on, then," she said. "I'll *get* there. Don't *worry*."

Rose Mercer shrugged.

"Come on, Retta," she said, and she and Loretta van Straten left the dormitory.

Ruth Bottomly stood to follow them. On the threshold, however, this latter stopped and sighed, her rib cage lifting her great, fat shoulders about her ears.

When the air had finished seeping out of her again, she said, "You okay, Plain? I mean, last night, you didn't

187

even come to *supper.* Is everything okay?"

She didn't turn back to say it. She spoke as though she were talking to somebody else, to some invisible third person, or to herself, perhaps.

Jane concentrated on the tilted reflection of her tie in a looking glass.

Ruth said, "Plain?"

"What *is* it?" said Jane, tugging at the silky, striped material, making the knot too tight, too small, praying that Ruth would hurry up and go, before. . . .

Before what?

It didn't matter what. Just, go. Not stand there with her shoulders hunched and her voice subdued, as though something unusual had happened, as though this morning weren't the same as every other morning.

With the toes of one foot, Jane extracted her shoes from beneath her bedside chair. First the right, then the left, she wriggled into them.

"For goodness' sake," she said, "stop hanging around for me. At the rate *you* move, I'll've caught up with you in five seconds anyway."

It was the strangeness of Ruth's waiting that angered her. It kept reminding her of something else; or, rather, threatening to remind her of something else, some dream that she'd had.

A bright, sharp-edged rectangle of sunlight fell through the dormitory window and warmed the dormitory floor. The air was fragrant with the smell of grilling bacon. Somewhere, in the beech woods beyond the grounds, probably, birds sang. It was Wednesday. The first lesson of the morning would be English. They'd be reading *Pride and Preju-*

dice, which Jane loved; yet still Ruth Bottomly shuffled with her back to her in the doorway and the incongruity of this persistent presence, its lack of apparent reason, stirred cold, faint echoes in Jane's mind.

She dragged a brush through her hair, noticing that it was more tangled than usual, but refusing to remember why. She only knew that she had to hurry. She must get to chapel. Chapel, breakfast, English and the certain, imminent pleasure of Darcy's proposal to Elizabeth.

She threw down her brush. She tugged at the cuffs of her shirt.

"Come on, then," she said, pushing past Ruth and out into the corridor. "Come on, Bummly. We're going to have to run."

Down the empty, wooden staircase they sped, she first, Ruth following. Reaching the ground floor, they swung right, crossed the entrance hall to the open front door, ran over gravel, under the archway, into the courtyard, and arrived at the foot of the chapel stairs as the prefect, on the top step, was about to close the heavy, carved pine door.

"*Get* up here. *Get* inside."

With the heel of her hand between their shoulder blades, the prefect pushed them, one after the other, into the nearest pew.

Behind them, the music mistress had begun to squeeze from an asthmatic harmonium the introductory bars to "New Every Morning." Around them, in row upon blue-sweatered row, faces to the altar, mouths ajar, the school stood waiting for the pause that would tell them to fill their lungs, stretch wide their nostrils and sing.

It came.

In a swooping glissando of assorted keys, they began:

"New every *mor-* orning *is* the *love*
Our *wa*kening *a-* and up*ri-* ising *prove . . .*"

Singing with them, one word in three, Jane peeled through the pages of a hymnbook.

"Hymn number four," whispered Ruth. "At the front. There. There. Number four."

". . . Res*tor*ed to *life* and *power* and *thought.*"

With a clearing of her throat, Jane sank into the familiar, senseless sounds, the communal thumping of rhythm, the communal gasps for breath.

Verse two was already starting:

"New mercies, each returning day,
Hover around us while we pray;
New perils past, new sins forgiven,
New thoughts of God, new hopes of Heav'n."

Jane had sung the hymn so often that she wasn't even conscious when one sentence ended and another began. Habit, with but an occasional clue from the book, shaped her lips. Habit lowered the pitch of her voice, then raised it. Towards the end of verse three, she allowed her gaze to drift from the printed page.

It was then that she saw Miss Anthony.

Standing on the low, wooden platform at the far end of the chapel, her back to the altar, her face to the school, her neat, colorless hands clasped in front of her stomach and her feet planted eighteen inches apart, the headmistress was waiting, as she did every weekday morning, for the singing to stop and the time for prayer to begin.

Jane saw her and she remembered.

Not with a shock; there was nothing violent about the way in which knowledge returned. There was no pain; only nausea; a dull, dulling heaviness; a furring-up of the stomach and throat, as she understood that the nightmare wasn't yet over, that neither sleeping nor waking again had ended it. Aziz was dead. She still hadn't told Miss Anthony.

The hatred of the evening before became irrelevant and useless. All over again, she must find the headmistress, must ask for permission to speak to her, must knock on the drawing-room door, enter, find the courage to say, "Please, I've got to tell you something. . . ."

Jane closed her hymnbook. She rested it on the narrow ledge in front of her. The singing had finished. She knelt, as, around her, eighty-nine other girls knelt, as, to her left, the half-dozen resident members of staff knelt, as the headmistress said, "Our Father, which art in Heaven . . ."

Jane tried to speak the words, more familiar to her than even those of the hymn, but the effort stuck in her throat.

She'd killed Miss Anthony's kitten. She'd really killed him. She'd committed murder and nobody, nobody in this chapel, knew what she'd done.

"Forgive us our tresspasses," they were saying, "as we forgive them that tresspass against us."

Miss Anthony was saying it. She was saying the words; but she didn't know, because Jane hadn't told her, what it was that she was asking her God to forgive.

"For Thine is the kingdom, the power and the glory. For ever and ever. Amen."

Ten minutes later, seated upright at her place in the dining room, half watching as Mrs. Bailey scooped bacon and tinned tomatoes from a shallow, metal dish, half listening to the chatter on her either side, Jane began to understand something else.

It wasn't just that she'd slept last night, and woken this morning, without having told Miss Anthony, but that she was going to sleep *every* night, wake *every* morning, without telling her.

24

She was never going to be able to tell Miss Anthony what she'd done. On her way from the chapel to the dining room, Jane had begun to plan the exact sentence she'd use when she managed to get her new interview with the headmistress, and it was then that she had understood that, even were she to find it, it would be useless.

For Miss Anthony wouldn't sit silent while Jane spoke, wouldn't, from silence, judge and pronounce sentence. She'd ask questions. However furious, however shocked and grief struck, she'd want to know, "How?"

Then, "What car? *Whose* car?"

And, as she passed along the table the plates of tomatoes and bacon that Mrs. Bailey had served, Jane knew that those were questions she could never answer. She hadn't the right to. She hadn't the right to impose, through *her* guilt, punishment on Gary; nor, through him, on Henrietta; nor, through Henrietta, on Audrey. She could guess what Audrey would suffer if she knew that her beloved sister's husband had driven, in secret, from London, to take Jane out for a drive. She wouldn't have to be told that he had kissed her. She'd sense the betrayal without that.

As for Gary himself, it occurred to Jane for the first time that, by having allowed her to drive his car on a public road, he might have done more than break the school rules, he might have committed a crime.

And, anyway, even if he hadn't, even if it were only that Henrietta and Audrey and Mrs. Croft found out what it was that he had done . . .

Now that they'd begun, the arguments wouldn't stop coming. Like tumbling bricks, they thundered into Jane's brain, each one entailing a dozen others, unstoppable.

"Excuse me, I've already got one."

"What?" asked Jane, aware, suddenly, of a hesitant voice at her elbow.

"I've already got a plate. I think this is yours."

"Oh," said Jane, "oh, sorry. I . . . Sorry, I didn't see."

She took back the plate that the first-former on her right was holding out to her. A rasher of bacon floated in a pool of tomato juice, the surface of which was flecked with disks of fat. She lowered the plate to the table.

When Gary had said, "I wish I knew if you were *capable* of coping," had this, then, been what he had meant? Not, could she cope with telling Miss Anthony, but could she cope with *not* telling her, with telling no one, with carrying her guilt unspoken, unshared, unpunished, inside her head forever? Jane remembered that he'd offered to come with her and talk to the headmistress, but saw that that had always been unthinkable.

193

She clenched her forehead. Like a many-headed serpent, the questions without answers twisted and thrashed in her skull.

She looked up to see whether anyone at the table had noticed, had spotted the chaos behind her eyes. She glanced at Mrs. Bailey, but the math mistress, having finished serving, was cutting the rashers of bacon that she'd left for herself into uniform, mouth-sized strips. When she'd finished the operation, she rested her knife on the rim of her plate, changed her fork to her right hand and, with a bored, mechanical gesture, pronged the strip nearest to her. She dabbled it in tomato juice before sliding it into her mouth.

Jane looked at Ruth, who, head bent, thick fringe obscuring her eyes, was also eating.

Everyone was eating. Slurp, slurp; munch, munch; cheeks swollen; jaws grinding; tongues darting out to make sure that nothing was missed, they ate as though it were the only thing that mattered, as though even the quality, the nature of the food was unimportant, beside the act of shoveling it in.

In a break for a mouthful of tea, a girl sitting opposite Jane caught her eye. For a moment, the two looked at each other, then, puzzled, embarrassed by the intensity of Jane's staring, the second girl withdrew. But she hadn't seen anything *frightening*, that was obvious. She hadn't seen the death inside Jane's head.

At last, Ruth lifted her face from the skeleton white of her plate, wiped her red mouth on her wrist, looked at Jane and said, "Don't tell me you're on a diet."

"No. I just don't feel hungry. D'you want it?"

"But you didn't even have any supper last night."

Jane realized that this was true. She hadn't eaten a thing since lunch the previous day. Nor was it, now, that she felt full, or sick, or physically incapable of eating. It was just that, away to her left, at the top table, Miss Anthony was smiling at something two girls were telling her and that, all through the dining room, bread was being buttered, was being spread with marmalade and devoured by people who didn't know that Aziz was dead.

"I don't blame you, mind you. It was pretty revolting."

"What?" said Jane. "*What* was? What're you talking about?"

With an outstretched hand, Ruth indicated her empty, shining plate.

"This muck," she said.

"Oh, yes," said Jane. "Well . . ."

Then Mrs. Bailey called, "Aren't you eating, Jane? All right. Well, pass your plate up to the end then. Has everyone finished? Good. Let's get this table cleared, shall we?"

No, quite obviously Jane's face was revealing nothing. There was no brand of shame on her forehead. If only there *had* been. If only . . .

She must tell the headmistress.

But she couldn't. She knew why she couldn't.

But what if the Termite *knew*, if the body'd been found, if someone had seen what had happened and told her.

What if the Termite *never* knew?

Jane's head burned. She felt as though it were about to ignite, to explode.

Ruth was saying, ". . . hear what Valerie called us, when we came thundering up the stairs to chapel this morning? Did you? Plain, did you? Did you hear what she said?"

195

"What *who* said?"

Jane was sure that she must have shouted the question, but, if she had, there was no reflection of this on Ruth's face, or in the chatty, impatient tone of her voice.

"Valerie Creighton. Didn't you hear what she said to us? She said, 'Have you no respect for God's house, you blasphemers?' You must've heard her. Haven't you noticed that, how they all become like nuns the moment they're on chapel duty?"

"I suppose so."

"They do. They get that sort of pious, squint-eyed look on their faces and whisper, even when they're yelling at you."

Jane laughed. She heard herself laugh, astonished, bewildered, frightened by the sound of her own amusement.

Her existence seemed to have split into two, one half remaining trapped and desperate inside her head, the other pursuing a calm, unremarkable onward passage through time.

And not only through breakfast, but all through that day, her two realities maintained their separate existence. Jane slipped from one to the other with frightening ease.

In English, she not only followed the story of *Pride and Prejudice* as, one page per girl, it was read out loud around the classroom, but became involved in it, took delight in it, in Elizabeth's happiness, Lady Catherine's anger, Mrs. Bennet's confusion.

At lunch, when it was announced that a girl from the fourth form had won second prize in an interschool painting competition, she clapped like everyone else; not only clapped, but felt pleased, as though such events were still relevant to her.

She didn't eat, however. As she was lifting the first fork-ful of meat and potatoes to her mouth, her hand froze as though of its own volition, then lowered itself and returned the food to the plate. It wasn't that she wasn't hungry; it was more as though her body knew that only by remaining in control of this, its eating, could it keep insanity at bay.

Walking up the drive to the games field, however, later that afternoon, with Miranda Spurling bouncing beside her and Simone de Preville on the far side of Miranda, Jane suddenly believed that the struggle was about to end. Here, in this place, on the school drive, she was sure that her two realities must meet, at last, and explode. Reaching the turnstile through which they must pass to get to the lacrosse pitch, she stopped. She had to stop. Heart thudding, lips cold and swollen, she touched Miranda's elbow.

"Yes?" asked Miranda, her round, freckled face empty of either crossness or suspicion.

Jane looked at her.

She tried to say, she *wanted* to say, "Can't we just walk on a bit farther? There're skid marks on the drive, just around the bend, and, somewhere in the hedge, there's the body of the Termite's kitten. . . ."

But she couldn't. She could only stare and wish, wish that Miranda would understand without being told; that *someone* would understand, for God's sake, and silence, one way or another, the questions and doubts that screeched inside her head.

Should she tell Miss Anthony?

Yes, of course, she must.

No, she *couldn't.*

"What is it, Plain?"

197

"What?" said Jane. "Oh, I . . . I . . . Sorry, Randy, I just . . ."

It wasn't going to happen.

She would say nothing. Miranda would see nothing.

"I'm sorry," she said. "I've forgotten."

Miranda laughed and shook her head.

Simone said, "Get on, zen, you two. I'm fweezing, standing awound here."

They moved on.

At breakfast on the following day, Thursday, Miss Anthony announced to the school that Aziz was missing.

"I know that some of you, particularly the junior girls, have been rather anxious about him," she said, "but you must all realize that cats aren't like dogs. They're independent little creatures and sometimes they do wander off, for days at a time. Now, I must ask you all *not* to worry. He'll turn up again, I promise you. You've all heard the expression about a cat having nine lives, haven't you? Well, I really don't think Aziz is old enough to have got through even *half* that number, do you?"

She smiled her thin, gray smile.

The school, uncertain, but obedient, laughed.

In a dizziness of terror, Jane pushed back her chair, began to stand, began to wave one arm in the air, but her movement and its noise were camouflaged by the sudden resumption of talking and eating around them. Jane sat again. She pushed her chair forward beneath the table's ledge. She watched, until it had died, the trembling of her wrists and of her hands.

25

"Plain, you're the nearest. Turn it off, will you?"

"Okay," said Jane.

She placed the book she'd been reading face downwards on her desk, stood up and reached across to silence the fifth-form radio. For the last half hour, it'd been playing a program of song requests. Now, the anchorman had announced a discussion on nuclear disarmament, which threatened not to be amusing.

"Thank goodness for that," said Ruth Bottomly, hunched over her desk at the front of the courtyard classroom. "Some of us are trying to review, you know."

"What you don't know now, there's no point learning," said Rose Mercer, quoting every member of staff who'd taught them over the past few days.

It was twenty past eight on Sunday evening. Aziz had been missing for five days now, but what conjecture there'd been, in the fifth-form classroom, as to the reason for his disappearance or the likelihood of his return, had already been superseded by the more urgent subject of the forthcoming "mock" General Certificate of Education exams. The first one, French, was to take place the following morning.

"Que je fusse, que tu fusses, qu'il ou elle fusse," read Jane, from the worn, thumbed, blue-covered book in front of her. Whether she learned them, the verbs, or whether she passed the exam, was a matter to which she was indifferent, but so

long as her brain could be satisfied with grammar and vocabulary and spelling, she was happy to let it be.

And it seemed as though it could. More and more, for longer and longer periods, she was finding it possible to drift on the school's easy flow, to forget, to accept the reflection of herself that the other girls, in their ignorance, held up for her. The only trouble was, that each time that memory *did* return, it was worse. Not more acute, but deeper and uglier and more desperate.

"That's one of the stupidest things I've ever heard," said Ruth, who was famous for being able to grip an argument as a bullterrier grips a rat. "It's what I *do* know there's no point learning, not what I don't."

"Oh, shut up, Bummly," called Miranda Spurling, laughing.

"Anyway, this is meant to be free time, not prep," said Rose, confident, smug, now that she had an ally.

Simone, who, her long legs dangling, was perched with Miranda on the top of a radiator, began to sing one of the songs that had just been played on the radio.

"No, come *on*," said Fiona Curtis, a pale, carroty girl who was new to the school that year. "That's not fair. After all, French *is* your own language, Prevy. Of course *you* don't need to review."

"Oh?" said Simone, pronouncing the word as though she were blowing a smoke ring. "Oh? Are you going to get a hundwed percent for English, zen?"

Ruth bellowed, "There *is* a difference of standards, if you don't mind my saying so. They're not just going to ask us things like what the bloody Duponts eat for *breakfast*, in the *English* paper. Are they?"

Simone laughed. Miranda, Rose and Loretta van Straten laughed with her.

"Watch it. You don't want Bummly losing her temper," said Jane.

The laughter swelled. Ruth had been known to break windows, furniture, even door panels when really enraged.

"Hey," said Simone, leaping down from the radiator. "I know. I want a game of cards. Where's Nicky and Augy?"

At once, Jane snapped her eyes back to the open pages of her book.

"Que nous fussions, que vous fussiez, qu'ils ou elles fussent."

She'd been caught off her guard. Audrey's name was one of the sounds that could reawake the horror dormant within her.

Two days before, on the Friday, they'd bumped into one another on the staircase and, to Jane's confusion, instead of behaving as though she hadn't seen her, Audrey had said, "Have you done that thing for the Termite yet? You know. That poem. That *poem* we had to learn, for putting on makeup on the train last weekend. Don't tell me you never went to *see* her about it."

"Oh, yes. Yes . . ."

"You should've seen her face when you didn't turn up after tea. Where the hell were you, anyway?"

"Nowhere. I just . . ."

Jane had not only been *puzzled* at Audrey's standing there, talking to her, talking about the weekend as though she'd forgotten what it had meant, but *frightened*. What game was Audrey playing? What trap was she setting?

"What poem was it, anyway?" she'd asked.

"Don't you even *know*?"

"No. I was supposed to ask you, but . . . I don't know. I just forgot."

Then Audrey, too, had looked puzzled and Jane's fear had increased. That everyone else should ignore the death in her, should behave towards her as though she were still one of them, was hard enough to bear, but that Audrey, who, whether she wanted it or not, whether she was conscious of it or not, was inextricably woven into that death, should ignore it was terrible.

Why couldn't she at least have retained her former distance? Why couldn't *she,* even if no one else could, even if Miss Anthony couldn't, sense what Jane had done? Why was she torturing Jane by trying to go back, when she *must* know, must be able to *see*, that it was now far, far too late?

Clenching jaws, fists, forehead, Jane forced her attention back to the French grammar. She must pretend to be working. She must pretend to herself that she was working. Within her brain, the questions were beginning to raise their insatiable heads and she *had* to lull them to sleep.

But her ears, oversensitive to the subject matter, couldn't stop listening to the dangerous voices around her.

From her post by the radiator, Simone was saying, "Where've zey *gone* to, zose two? Augy and Nicky? Not off to ze telephone box again?"

"I should think so."

That was Rose Mercer.

"Zey're mad. Zey're going to get caught if zey cawy on like zat."

"Serve 'em damn well right."

That, of course, was Ruth.

"Oh, shut up!"

Those were a dozen assorted voices around the room.

"Hey, Plain!"

Now it was Miranda speaking. Her buoyant voice landed, quivering, on the rim of Jane's desk.

"Plain!"

"Yes," said Jane, fighting to stay in her book.

"Didn't they tell *you* where they were going?"

"No. I don't know anything about it," she said.

"Go on, I bet you do. Who're they ringing up? Nicky's actor boyfriend?"

"Honestly, Randy, I don't know."

What was the *matter* with them? Was it really ignorance that made them keep on mentioning Audrey, the telephone box? Could they really not see the link between those and Aziz's disappearance?

Or *could* they? Could the whole school see it? Did the whole school know that she'd committed murder and was it waiting, breathless, for the moment when she'd break down and confess?

Why didn't she do it now, then?

She could. She could stand up, there, in the fifth-form classroom, and scream, "I did it! I ran him over. I *killed* him," over and over, louder and louder, until her brain exploded and the soft, silent shreds bespattered the white-washed walls.

Then it'd be over. It'd be up to them to clean the mess; not her. She, at last, would be able to rest.

The chapel clock sounded half past eight. The door of the

classroom opened. Audrey and Nicky walked in.

"Zere you are, you cweeps. Where've you been? Wandy and I are wanting a game of cards."

"Have you been to the telephone box? Did anyone see you?"

"You know you'll be in the most awful trouble if you get caught."

"Oh, shut up. Don't be so *pathetic*."

It was Audrey who spoke, and something in her voice, in the way in which she spat the word "pathetic," in the way in which she strode across the classroom, sat at her desk, flung open the lid of her desk and extracted the first book upon which her hand alighted, silenced, for a moment, the whole class.

Jane, too, was shocked. The despair with which she'd been struggling a minute before released its hold. Frowning, unaware she was closing the blue French grammar book, she looked at Audrey. For a moment, she thought that she was looking into a mirror.

"Sorry I spoke, I'm sure," said Rose, from the middle of the silence.

Miranda said, "Don't you want to play cards, then, Augy? There's still quarter of an hour till bed."

Audrey didn't reply.

Nicky said, "*I*'ll play."

Jane swung to look from Audrey to Nicky. She hadn't focused on anyone this clearly for days. She saw the girl's pale face, her slim, arched eyebrows, her twisted, sneering upper lip and felt an inexplicable anger electrify her nerves.

Where it had come from, this surprising emotion, she

couldn't begin to imagine, nor could she even be sure that it was Nicky who'd evoked it, or something in Audrey, something that she'd seen, and recognized, in Audrey's eyes.

But when Simone said, "We'll play with just ze swee of us, zen. But, what's up wiz your fwiend?" she felt it charge through her again with redoubled power.

"I've absolutely no idea what's up with her," said Nicky. "Maybe she just doesn't like poker anymore. Maybe she'd prefer a game of *snap*, or snakes and ladders. Who can tell?"

Although nobody knew what she meant, someone laughed. Miranda said, "Well, what about you, Plain? Will you play with us?"

"No thank you," said Jane.

She said it without thinking, without even knowing what it was that she was going to answer. In this silly, insidious quarrel that had nothing to do with her, to whose outcome she was indifferent, she'd automatically taken Audrey's side. Why, for heaven's sake? Why take anybody's side? Why get involved at all? As though hoping to find the explanation there, she looked back across the gangway to Audrey's desk.

"What's ze matter?" called Simone. "Checking to see whezzer zat's okay wiz your fwiend?"

Miranda said, "Come on, Plain. It's much more fun with four. Honestly."

"Oh, leave her," said Nicky. "Plain's just doing one of her famous I've-got-to-work-or-I'll-fail-tomorrow's-exam acts. You know the ones I mean. Invariably followed by the

what-a-terrible-paper-I-don't-think-I-got-one-answer-right
act, then the good-heavens-ninety-percent-how-incredible
act. Isn't that it? Aren't I right, Plain?"

"No," said Jane, a strange dizziness numbing her
thoughts, paralyzing her logic.

"Oh, of course I am," said Nicky. "You're transparent,
Plain."

"And you're . . ."

"What? What am I? Oh, come on, don't tell me that
wonderful vocabulary's gone and run out on you."

"You're stupid, Nicky, that's what you are."

"*Stupid*? Is that the best you can do?"

"It's the truth. You and Simone and Rose and . . ."

Jane didn't mean to carry on, wasn't even sure what she
was saying, but the words could not be stopped.

"Just because you've got sharper tongues and bigger
mouths than everybody else, that's no reason to assume you
rule the damn *world*. You come in here, you trample over
everybody's feelings. . . . I mean, there *are* people, not me,
but other people, who're genuinely trying to review. Do you
think it's funny that they can't, because you're so busy
being loud and arrogant and creasing each other up with
your so-called wit? Do you? Because, let me tell you, it's
not. It's stupid and ridiculous and infantile, if you want to
know."

She was standing, by now, had moved out from between her desk and her chair, into the gangway. Her feet
were planted apart and her fists were raised to the level of
her hips, as though she were waiting for a fight. A long
way away from her, at the end of a dark tunnel, Nicky,
Simone and the others had merged into one person, but it

wasn't really at them that she was shouting.

"And do you know why you're so ridiculous? Let me tell you. It's . . . It's . . . It's because you think you're so damn *big*. So *big*. Lounging around with your feet on the desks, playing poker, listening to the radio at full volume, making cheap jokes about anyone who tries to assert her right to the classroom. You do, you think you're goddamn *lordlings*. But just look around, will you? Look at the world you think you rule over. Can't you see how small and unimportant it is? I mean, a real person'd just tread it into the ground without noticing, wouldn't even feel it under her foot, honestly. But I don't think you even know real people exist. I don't think you'd know real thoughts, or feelings, or . . . or problems, if you saw them, if your smug, silly faces were rubbed *into* them. You wouldn't. I know you wouldn't. You're such *children*. So . . . So get on with your game of cards and leave me alone. Leave Audrey alone. You make me sick. The lot of you make me sick, as a matter of fact. The whole damn lot of you."

With shaking, uncurling fingers, Jane groped through darkness for her chair. Around her, silence held its breath.

Jane touched the chair. She felt the smoothness of its curved, varnished back, the steadiness of it, the stability of it beneath the weight in her arm.

Then the silence began to crumble. Lungs released their air. Bodies creaked into motion and someone said, "Well!"

"You're telling *me*, well."

"Whoof! That's put *us* in our place, hasn't it?"

"What do you suppose bwought zat on?"

"God knows."

But Jane hardly heard them, the voices. As she slid her

hand down the upright of the chair's back, as she found its seat, as she sat on it, she'd already forgotten what had caused them. In her brain there was only one thought, one knowledge, one certainty. She knew what it was that she must do.

Part 7

26

Half an hour later, her dressing gown knotted around her, her green leather slippers half on, half off her feet, Jane sat on a stool in a curtained bathroom cubicle and watched as yellowish water glugged from two wide-mouthed taps. There was a reason why the water in the school ran yellow, but she couldn't, for the moment, remember what. In the cubicle next to hers, someone was singing.

When the bath was a quarter full, Jane stood up and turned off the taps. Then she rolled back the right-hand sleeve of her dressing gown and, supporting herself with her left hand on the tub's edge, leaned over to splash and stir and agitate the water.

"Now, what are *you* up to? Not just *pretending* to wash, I hope. I'm surprised at you, Jane, that's usually a first-form trick."

Jane closed her eyes. It was the jollier of the two under-matrons. Jane closed her eyes and tried to close her ears.

"Come on. In you get. It'll be lights out in a quarter of an hour."

Jane opened her eyes.

"Yes, all right," she said.

"Hurry up, then. You can't bathe with your dressing gown on, can you?"

"No," said Jane.

She unknotted the cord and slid the woolen dressing gown from her shoulders.

"That's better," said the under-matron. Then, "Good heavens, girl, what *have* you been up to? Those *ribs* on you! Jane, look at me. You're not dieting, or something, are you?"

"Of course not," said Jane, crouching in the shallow, tepid water.

"I'm afraid I don't believe you, poppet. I know you've never been *fat*, but this is ridiculous. You *can't* have been eating properly."

"I have," said Jane.

If only the woman would go. If only she knew how much less than her *Aziz* had been eating, how thin *he* must be, with his fur flattened against his bones, his flesh wasted.

"Honestly," she said, "I'm not thin. I'm all right. Honestly."

"Protest as much as you want, but I'm not blind, I'm afraid. You're going to have to come along to the infirmary tomorrow morning, before breakfast, to get weighed. This really can't go on. And what's *that*, for heaven's sake? On your arm? What *have* you been doing to yourself?"

"It's nothing," said Jane. "I don't . . . It's nothing."

"Well, you just remember to come along to the infirmary

212

tomorrow. I'll be waiting for you. I shan't forget."

"Okay," said Jane.

Anything, so long as the under-matron would leave her now.

"You won't forget? Very well. Now, hurry up and get washed. It's almost time for bed."

With a swish of white cotton curtains, a rattle of rings on railing, the under-matron left. Jane crouched as she was for several minutes.

From the distraction of the woman's stupid and uninformed worry, she sifted back to the one important truth. When she held this once more in her head, when, once more, her thoughts were moving in the right direction, she removed the plug, climbed out of the bath, tugged on her pajamas, her dressing gown, her slippers and walked back along the corridor to her dormitory.

As she did so, the bell for lights out rang.

"Night!" called someone, from an open dormitory doorway.

"Night!" answered someone else.

"Hey! What time're you getting up to review tomorrow?"

"I don't know. What about you?"

"All right girls, no more talking. To your own rooms now. Come along. Quick, quick. Into bed all of you."

Having removed her dressing gown and slippers and hung them over her chair, Jane eased herself between her sheets.

"Is everyone in here ready? Come on, Loretta, in you get now. Your hair's been brushed quite enough. All right, everyone. Now, no more talking. All right? Good night."

"Night."

"Good night."

"Good night."

The dormitory door banged shut onto darkness. The under-matron's footsteps, her jovial, hectoring voice, faded away to a murmur. Then, as the gray rectangle of light from the window began to increase its power, the darkness in the dormitory slid back to reveal, once again, chests o' drawers, chairs, clothes, wash jugs and faces.

Loretta and Rose were leaning across the gap between their respective beds, giggling.

Closer to Jane, with a creaking of mattress springs, Ruth hauled her weight onto one elbow.

"Nice bath?"

Jane knew to whom she was speaking, but pretended not to have heard.

"Augy was in here earlier, looking for you."

Jane's lips parted. She almost said, "Why? What did she want?"

Instead, however, she clamped her lips shut, clenched her forehead, her eyes, forcing herself to concentrate on the one important thought.

"I told her it was your bath night. Did she come and see you? Did she? Plain, did Augy get to see you? Plain!"

"No," whispered Jane, on a hiss.

"Oh. Oh, well, I don't know what she wanted. I don't know if it was important, or anything."

"I shouldn't *think* so."

"I don't know. She didn't say. Hey!"

In a second eruption of creaking and puffing, Ruth heaved her body still farther out of its bed.

"Hey, by the way, well done for what you said to Nicky

214

and Prevy this evening. That was pretty terrific, if you don't mind my saying so. Plain! Plain?"

"Yes, okay. I heard."

"Well it was. It was time someone put them in their place and you did it jolly well."

Jane sat up.

"Stop going *on* about it," she said. "You don't know the first . . . Look, please Ruth, will you just let me get to sleep? Will you stop talking and let me get to sleep? Okay? I'm sorry, but I . . . I'm just tired, that's all. Okay?"

"Okay," said Ruth, gathering to her bosom the pieces of her broken dignity, maneuvering her body back beneath the blankets. "I don't mind."

Jane lowered her head once again to her pillow. But she'd no intention of sleeping. She was listening.

Five or six minutes later, she heard what it was she'd been waiting for: a deceleration, a loss of power and intensity in the giggling, at the other end of the room, between Rose and Loretta. Gaps, each longer than the last, had begun to appear in the sibilant conversation. Between the gaps, the words had begun to stumble, to stagger, to revive with a start, then stagger and stumble again. At last, like moths, they died. Silence slipped into their place. But still Jane waited.

It wasn't until the silence itself had been replaced, by the rhythmic gurgle and wheeze of Ruth's snoring, that she sat up, pushed back her blankets, twisted her hips around and lowered her feet to the floor. Then, carefully, steadily, testing each board with her toes, she crossed the space between her bed and Ruth's. She moved in time with Ruth's snoring, which was how, so her father'd once told her, housebreak-

215

ers always moved. At the edge of Ruth's bed, she stopped. She reached down and touched the pillow. The fat, red face below her contracted for a second, then relaxed.

Jane breathed. She bent at the knees and waist. She slithered her hand beneath Ruth's pillow, keeping it as flat as she could, groping, feeling with her fingertips alone.

At last she found it. At last, she found the warm, smooth, plastic body of Ruth's flashlight. Holding her eyes all the time on its owner's face, Jane tapped the flashlight, wriggled it, pushed it and drew it towards herself.

It was free. It was in her hand. She had it.

Releasing her breath in a long, silent judder, she straightened up. She crossed to the dormitory door without going back for either her slippers or her dressing gown.

There, she stopped again and listened. Then, hearing nothing but the steady snoring behind her, the softer, steady breathing of Rose and Loretta, she gripped the handle, pulled the door's resistance towards her, turned the handle, opened the door and stepped out of the dormitory onto the dimly lit landing.

It was then, in that second of readjustment, that Jane thought that she saw something, some movement, some thickening of shadow upon shadow at the far end of the corridor and her heart crashed into her stomach. But no one spoke. No loud voice shattered the silence with "Jane Rackham! Where on *earth* do you think *you're* going?"

She lessened her grip on the flashlight and carried on.

27

This time, she was going to find his body.

No matter that five days had passed since last she'd tried and failed; no matter that it was a cloud-thick, starless night and that Ruth's flashlight threw only a pencil-thin beam ahead of her along the school drive; this time, she would find it. She had to.

To find Aziz's body, to dig a grave for him and to bury him was the only atonement left to Jane. She couldn't bring him back to life. Without convicting innocent people, she couldn't confess to his murder. That she must do *something*, however, before her brain cracked beneath the weight of the guilt it bore, she'd known now for several hours.

And, already, as she swung the beam of Ruth's flashlight from side to side through the thick, silent mist, peering for the skid marks that'd tell her where to begin her search, the raw coldness of her feet, hands, wrists and face was beginning to lighten the guilt. It was *right* that she'd come as exposed to the night as Aziz was, that grit cut the soles of her feet and that her pajama legs flapped damp around her ankles. She *knew* that it was right and she *knew* that she would find him.

Ten minutes later, however, Jane still hadn't managed to identify, among the myriad blemishes and illusions of blemishes with which night had disguised the drive's surface, the skid marks that she needed in order to begin.

"Come *on*," she said; although, this time, there was no

deadline. This time, Jane had not only the whole night, but for as long as it took, to find Aziz's body. There was nothing else that she had to do. There was nowhere else that she had to go.

Though the beam of Ruth's flashlight was being absorbed by the carpet of ground mist it should've been piercing, though her fingers around the flashlight's body were aching and raw, she didn't care. All that mattered was that she was doing something, was moving, was moving *towards* the nightmare, not struggling and twisting away from it.

"Come on, Aziz," she said. "I'm going to find you, darling. I promise."

She made herself walk more slowly, investigate each clue more thoroughly. Success, not speed, was important now. Nor was it important that her feet had become too cold to feel where the gravel sliced them. So long as they continued to carry her, to support her, she could ignore the rest.

"Aziz! Where are you, boy? I'm going to find you!"

Then, through a split in the cloud, moonlight poured down and soaked the drive with its whiteness. Straightening up, seeing, a few yards ahead of her, the twin sentinel gateposts, the main road, Jane realized that she'd wandered too far.

She turned. The cloud closed again. But, in the instant before it did so, Jane became aware, for the second time that night, of another presence than hers, of another held breath, another poised momentum troubling the shadows.

She froze.

Through the galloping of blood in her ears, she strained to hear it again: the sound that wasn't of wind, or of undergrowth, or of scurrying nocturnal animals.

218

In the rigid, quivering beam of Ruth's flashlight, she strained to see the shape that didn't belong.

All thought and intention had left her. Only this, the muscles stretched to breaking point, the saliva trickling into the bowl of her half-open mouth, the scream bunched to spring, remained.

"Plain?"

Darkness dived into her lungs.

"It's okay! It's only me, you idiot."

"Who . . . ?"

With the thin, blind blade of her flashlight, she lashed at the blackness.

"Me! It's Augy! For goodness' sake . . ."

Fingers grabbed Jane's wrist, twisted it upwards, twisted the light beam up with it.

"Augy," said Jane, but her voice choked on its unreleased scream. She could see Audrey's face now, could feel her hand's solidity, yet the fear remained clawing and trapped inside her throat.

"Yes," said Audrey, "it's only me. What did you think?"

"I . . ."

Jane gasped. She swung her head to one side. Then, shivering, convulsed, helpless, she began to laugh.

"What's the matter?"

"Nothing," she said.

"Come on! Stop it. Plain, stop it. Tell me what the hell you're doing out here. Have you gone mad or something?"

"No. No, I . . ."

"You're not running *away*?"

"No . . ."

The laughter was no longer a release. It was beginning to

219

hurt, like vomiting on an empty stomach. Yet Jane couldn't stop. Not only her diaphragm, but her whole body jerked and contracted with the uncontrollable force.

"For God's sake, Plain, someone'll hear us."

"Who?"

The laughter increased.

"Okay. Okay, but shut up now, will you? I'm sorry if I scared you, but, honestly, what on earth're you doing out here? And look at you, you must be freezing. *I* am. And I've got my dressing gown on, at least. Here, give me that flashlight. If you're going to keep waving it around like some demented lighthouse keeper . . ."

"I'm sorry," said Jane, as their hands touched once more, as Audrey's removed from hers the flashlight, then shot its light in her face.

"Don't," she said, screwing her eyes shut, feeling the laughter skid to a halt in her stomach. "Don't *do* that."

The flashlight clicked off. Jane opened her eyes. In a second or two, Audrey's features returned to her, darker than before and less defined, but easier, now, to understand.

"Okay?" asked Audrey.

"Yes," said Jane. "Yes."

"Thank God for that."

Jane said, "I suppose that was you, earlier, on the landing outside the dorms."

"I didn't think you'd seen me. Yeah. I was just coming to talk to you. Then when I saw you creeping off down the stairs like some old villain . . . Look, what the hell're you playing at, Plain Face?"

"Oh," said Jane.

She dropped her gaze, then lifted it and swung it away,

over the mottled, silver-gray shadowings of hedges, fields, trees and clouds. The cold was closing back in on her, like armor.

"Oh?" said Audrey. "Oh? What the hell's *that* supposed to mean?"

Jane said, "What?"

"For goodness' sake!"

Jane heard Audrey jab at the drive with one slippered foot, heard her turn immediately afterwards, as though she were about to leave, as though she were about to stride back into the night, to thicken, darken and cease, once more, to exist. And wasn't that what Jane *wanted* her to do?

"Look . . ." she said.

"Yes?"

"It's . . ."

She searched for Audrey's face and found it again. It was a quarter twisted away from her; the chin was hidden behind a dressing gown's hunched shoulders; but she could see that the eyebrows were tight, that the plump lips were swollen and sulking and that, on either side of the forehead, hung bedraggled curtains of hair.

She raised one hand, as though to touch the face, then eased it back to its position by her side.

"Well?" asked Audrey. "What were you going to say?"

Jane shaped her mouth around silence. She couldn't even remember what it was that she'd been asked.

"Go on."

"I . . ." she said.

"Go on. It can't be *that* awful, whatever it is, whatever you're up to. I mean . . ."

Then Jane said, "Oh, God, Augy!"

28

"Oh God, Augy!" she said and, as the words burst out of her, as they exploded out of her, defeat stood up from where it must have been waiting all along and strolled inside to take, at last, its place. Almost painlessly, almost kindly, the final hope had collapsed.

It was over. The delusion of strength that had carried her forth on her search, the delusions of atonement, of a final, grand solution, lay now exposed and ridiculous alongside her bare, swollen feet on the drive.

"Okay, Plain, take it easy," said Audrey, approaching, touching Jane's shoulder, curling one arm about Jane's shoulders and drawing her towards herself. "Take it easy."

Defenseless, mindless, Jane allowed Audrey's warmth to absorb the worst of her shivering.

"Come on, tell me. Tell me, Plain. What is it? What's the matter? It's not . . ."

"Aziz," said Jane, and the fact that she could pronounce his name out loud, when, for the past five days, it had tortured her merely to hear someone *else* pronounce it, confirmed for her the totality of her collapse.

"What on earth're you talking about? Plain? What d'you mean, 'Aziz'?"

"His body's out here somewhere. I came to find it."

"How d'you . . . ? I mean, what d'you *mean*? What d'you *mean* his body's out here?"

"It just is," said Jane. "Because I *killed* him. *That*'s how

222

I know, so . . . Augy, I killed him. The Termite doesn't know, but . . . I hit him, in a car, driving a car. He ran out in front of the car and I didn't know how to stop, or . . . He's dead, Augy. He's somewhere out here and I've got to find him."

She'd pulled away from Audrey, but the two were still holding each other; as though the night were a sea that might drown them both, it seemed to Jane. Might drown them *both*? Yes, why was Audrey still clutching her arm? Why hadn't she dropped it, in horror, or disbelief, or scorn?

She said, "Don't you understand what I'm telling you? Don't you *believe* me?"

"Yes," said Audrey.

"What?"

"Yes."

"Then . . . ?"

"Look," said Audrey. "Look, Plain, I mean, how do you *know* you killed him?"

"What?"

"How do you *know*?"

"I just do, Augy. You've got to believe me."

"All right. But . . ."

Then Audrey said, "It wasn't that day you skipped off games, was it? You know, the day we were both supposed to go and see the Termite and you didn't turn up?"

"Yes," said Jane, puzzled, taken aback, not only by the change of subject, but by something that she wasn't understanding in Audrey's voice. She remembered, too, how strange had been Audrey's conduct earlier that evening, when she'd come back from the telephone box with Nicky; how remote she'd seemed, how . . .

How *what*?

"Yes," she said, "that was when it happened. Why?"

But she was no longer certain what it was that they were talking about.

"I don't know," said Audrey. "I just wondered. You've been so . . . Well, I know it's partly my fault, really. I mean, you know, that stupid fight we had in the basement and all that. . . ."

"Oh, that," said Jane.

"Yes," said Audrey. "Well . . ."

For a moment, they were both silent. Above them, thick cloud folded over thick cloud and a fox barked, away to the north.

"Anyway," said Audrey, at last, "that's sort of what I was coming to see you about, before, in the dorm. You know, to say I was sorry if I hurt you. . . . Against the locker, you know . . . and . . ."

"Oh, come on, it was *my* fault," said Jane. "You know it was."

"Well, thank you, anyway, for sticking up for me this evening in the classroom and so on. . . ."

"I didn't really. I mean . . ."

"She can be such a *bastard*."

Jane didn't have to ask to know that the "she" was Nicky. Nor, for reasons that she couldn't yet explain, was Audrey's curious reaction to her confession upsetting her. On the contrary, there was something in it, in the troubled, disjointed tone of it, that was sounding inside her brain like the high, sweet, almost inaudible notes of a promise.

"In what particular way, a bastard?" she asked.

Audrey said, "Oh . . ."

"You don't have to tell me if you don't want to."

"No, I . . . Look, aren't you freezing? Why don't you put my dressing gown on for a bit?"

"Don't be stupid. I'm fine. What did she do, then? What's Nicky done?"

"Nothing. She . . . Plain, listen," said Audrey, grabbing through the dimness for Jane's left wrist.

She stared at Jane's face, her dark irises sweeping over forehead, nose, cheeks, mouth, as though she were seeing these things for the first time, as though, for the first time, she were trying to understand them.

"What is it?" asked Jane.

"It's Aziz," said Audrey, and the way that she spoke his name, not with the fat, self-indulgent sigh that others had used since the kitten's disappearance, but hard, sharp and desperate, made Jane gasp with recognition.

It was *pain* that she'd been hearing, all this time, in Audrey's voice, the same pain as that with which Jane had woken and slept and breathed for the last five days, the pain of knowledge, the pain of unsharable guilt. Why hadn't she known it sooner? Why hadn't *she*, of all people, identified it sooner?

Jane found that she was returning Audrey's stare, that her eyes were boring into Audrey's with a need that was like hunger. Their distance from each other had never, in a way, been greater, yet Jane felt herself fighting to cross it and knew, without knowing why, that Audrey was making the same, huge effort.

So that when Audrey said, "Listen, Plain, he isn't dead. At least . . . Plain, did you hear what I said? Aziz *isn't dead,*" she failed, at first, to react.

"Yes he is," she said.

"He's not! Plain, we saw him. That's what I'm trying to tell you. When Nicky and I were out at the phone box this evening, we *saw* him. He was up in Eliston's Woods. He looked terrible, all skinny and matted and, I don't know, I think there was something wrong with one of his legs. But it was *him*, I know.

"Nicky said it wasn't. Oh, we both said maybe it wasn't. We didn't want it to be, you see. I mean, you know, we weren't supposed to *be* there, for God's sake, and . . . Anyway, by the time we . . .

"Nicky just thought the whole thing was a joke. She said she was damned if *she* was going to get into trouble over a cat that didn't know how to look after itself. She said I was soft. She said I was pathetic like *you*, as a matter of fact. Going gooey over animals. She said what did I want to do? Slip a note under the Termite's door, saying, Your cat's in Eliston's Woods, signed a well-wisher? Or something infantile like that? He'd find his way back if he wanted to. Cats did. But, I mean, he'd obviously hurt himself and . . . I don't know, I just . . . Anyway, by the time I tried to catch him, he'd disappeared. Down a hole or something. Somewhere. I don't know, I . . ."

Audrey's eyes slid away from Jane's face. Her right hand uncurled itself from Jane's wrist and sought the right-hand pocket of her dressing gown. Once it was safe inside, she shrugged and said, "Well, I just couldn't find him and . . . Well . . ."

For a time that seemed without measure, Jane stared at Audrey, seeing nothing, thinking nothing, feeling nothing.

226

Then, with a calmness that hardly surprised her, she said, "Which bit of the woods?"

"What?"

"Which *bit* of the woods, Aug?"

"What? Where we saw him?"

"Yes. Where *was* it?"

"Well, where the path goes. Just a bit in from the path . . ."

"Show me!"

29

And then they were moving. And then, as one, they were running towards the fence that bordered the drive. Neither Jane led nor Audrey. Side by side, they climbed the fence, paused, jumped down and stumbled to regain their balance among the thick, uneven grass.

"Hell," said Audrey, "I can't . . . Where is it? Where's the path, Plain? It all looks so different."

Jane said, "It must be back this way. Yes, look, down there, I'm sure it is. Come on."

Past startled sheep they ran together, without pause or need for comment. Once, when Audrey tripped on a hummock, staggered and almost fell, Jane relaxed to regain the lost balance as though it had been her own. The woods grew larger, closer.

From behind a panel of cloud, the moon slid out, dropped over the field, then slipped back again. A long way away, the chapel clock called one, two, three, four, all the way through to twelve. Jane heard it, even counted the long, quavering notes, but her mind had no use for the knowledge that was being sent. The woods were coming ever closer. The woods were almost upon them. Nothing mattered but that.

They'd reached the woods.

Suddenly, as though their arrival had involved no traveling, they were at the place where the path ended, were swaying on the edge of the path, at the entrance to a black, tree-enclosed tunnel. Their heart and lungs raced ahead of them, but their limbs had halted, awaiting the new instruction from their brain.

"Okay," said Jane. "Okay. Now where? Where exactly?"

But the words, squeezed out between gasps for breath, were unnecessary. Audrey'd already asked herself the same question, was already beginning to answer it, as she felt for Ruth's flashlight in her dressing-gown pocket, extracted the flashlight, clicked it on; as she raised its beam like a lance out in front of her.

"Now just," she said, taking one step into the tunnel. "Just . . ."

Again, the words were irrelevant. Jane understood. What nervousness Audrey was feeling, what numbness hung between hopelessness and hope, these were hers, too. If they spoke, it was only for the luxury of hearing their union stated, out loud, against the night.

Side by side then, hand brushing against back of hand, shoulder against shoulder, they began to walk forwards. Their hearing scanned the thickness around them, learning it, learning to analyze it. Their sight leaped from flashlight beam to darkness to flashlight beam. Their shivering rode hunched and still in their chest.

Step, after pause, after step, after pause, they moved forwards. They were halfway into the woods. Blackness and the rich, musky smell of leaf mold enveloped them.

Then Audrey said, "Somewhere around . . ."

"Here?"

"Yes, somewhere . . ."

And they stopped.

Undergrowth rustled. Thick branches creaked overhead.

"About here?" asked Jane.

"Yes, somewhere . . ."

Undergrowth rustled and, above their heads, like the floorboards of an empty house, thick branches creaked. The smell of leaf mold grew stronger.

They'd arrived.

Whether or not *this* place, rather than somewhere a few yards back, or a few yards on, was *the* place where Audrey and Nicky had seen a cat that may or may not have been the Termite's, they both knew that they'd arrived. Here, in the heart of Eliston's Woods, out of sight of the comfortable, gray, sheep-breathing field, out of sight of the road that bore lorries and cars and yellow-lit buses to London, their time had run out.

So that when, having clenched her toes around the cold, wet twigginess of the path, having licked her lips and cleared her throat, Jane called, "Aziz," the word stayed suspended about her head like smoke on a windless day, having nowhere forwards to go.

"Aziz."

"Aziz," called Audrey.

"Aziz."

They shouted together, their voice one voice, their emotion one nameless emotion.

Then

And then

And then, from the darkness, from the impenetrable thickness of undergrowth, bracken and ferns, from the echoing reverberation of their calling, he

Gray with dirt, dragging dead twigs behind him, hobbling and dragging behind him a stiff, useless leg, he

He came.

He came to them.

Through a previously unnoticed gap in the undergrowth, meowing, limping, tiny, matted and furious, he came to them.

Their voice died in their throat. Their breathing, their heartbeat grew slow. Together, they knelt, they extended their right hand, they rubbed the fingers of their right hand against the thumb.

"Here, boy," they whispered.

"Here, Aziz. Come here."

"Come here, boy. Here. Here, Aziz."

Suddenly, they might all three have been in the Termite's drawing room. Crouched on their haunches, feeling the strain in their thighs, watching the limping, erratic approach of the kitten, suddenly neither Jane nor Audrey could recall their emotion of a minute before. It had become unreal. It had become improbable. The present, the kitten's presence, was all that they now knew.

And when, at last, Jane touched Aziz, scooped her hand beneath his belly and lifted him up against her chest, although she cried, although tears soaked her face and the cotton collar of her pajamas, she was no longer able to imagine how it had been *without* him. That he was in her arms, that he was warm and hard and snuggling against her body, denied, not only his previous death, but *her* previous *suffering*.

She said, "Oh, God. Thank God. Oh, God," but the words, like the tears, flowed more from pleasure than from remembrance of pain.

"Careful of his leg," said Audrey.

She, too, was crying, or maybe laughing, the gasps from her diaphragm shaking the flow of her voice.

Jane said, "Yes, okay, he's okay. Have you got the flashlight?"

"Here," said Audrey.

"Shine it on him. Go on. On his leg. Can you see what's wrong with it?"

"I don't know. I think he might've broken it or something."

"Oh, God! But he couldn't't've walked, could he, if it was broken?"

"I don't know. Maybe it's just fractured. I'm not . . . Anyway, at least it can't be *too* serious, can it? I mean, you know, if he's managed to last . . ."

"God, Augy, he's awfully thin."

"Let me feel."

Audrey lowered the flashlight and stroked the cat's head, his rough, crusted coat, his swaying tail. A noise like sleepy, asthmatic breathing escaped from the animal's throat.

"For goodness' sake," she said. "Listen, Plain, he's purring."

The muscles of Jane's arms contracted and, although her

real grip on the kitten didn't change, in her mind, she crushed him against her chest.

"*That*'s not a bad sound, is it, old Plain Face?" said Audrey, smiling, shivering, replacing her hands in her pockets.

"No, it's . . . No, it jolly well isn't," said Jane.

From either side of the kitten, they looked at one another. In spite of the darkness, each found the other's face with ease. Jane saw that Audrey's hair lay flat against her head, that it was sticking to her forehead and to the sides of her face in ridiculous, black spikes. She saw that Audrey's parted lips were swollen and cracked with the cold. She saw that her nose ran and she realized that she loved her.

There was nothing urgent about the feeling. Rather was it soft, relaxed and slightly amused at itself. Nor was there anything to be expected from it. As it stood, it was complete.

"Your nose's running," she said, at last.

Audrey wiped her face with the back of her hand, then again with her dressing-gown sleeve.

When she'd finished, she said, "You should see yourself. You look awful. Almost worse than Aziz. Really."

"Do I?" said Jane. "Well . . ."

She shrugged. Then, bursting into laughter, she closed her eyes and lifted the kitten to rub his small, hard head against her own. She couldn't stop laughing and, now, Audrey was laughing with her, was laughing for the same reason, from the same idiotic happiness.

At last Jane managed to say, "Well . . . Well, now we've found him, we'd better get him back. Get him something to eat, some milk or something."

So off they set, back along the tree-roofed tunnel, moving fast through the cold, but without tension. When the path emerged from the woods into the gray, open sheep field, they broke their single file to walk side by side. Their feet pad-padded in unison. A sharp wind hurried them forwards, as though they were sailboats.

"Hey," said Jane.

"Hey what?" said Audrey.

"Hey . . . *everything*," she said.

Ten minutes later, they reached the school. While Jane restrained the excited, struggling kitten, Audrey eased open the heavy front door, her lips parted, her tongue licking the blade of her upper teeth.

"Okay. Come on."

Jane followed her in, into the entrance hall's stale, tepid darkness, into its humming silence, so oppressive after the noises of the night outside.

"Shhh, boy," she whispered to the frantic beast in her arms.

"Come on, let's go to the kitchen."

"Won't it be locked up?" she asked.

"No, of course not. You don't think anyone actually *wants* to eat that muck when they don't *have* to, do you?"

"No, I don't suppose they do," said Jane, laughing.

"Shhh," said Audrey. "Come on."

They reached the kitchen. They opened its door and entered. Jane closed its door. Audrey tiptoed to the fridge, removed a pint bottle of milk, looked around, saw a pie-dish and emptied the milk into that. She placed the pie-dish on the kitchen table. Jane walked to the table and stood the kitten by the milk.

"That's it," said Audrey. "You remember what *that* is, don't you? There. Look at him. Look at him, Plain."

"I know. He seems to be managing on his leg, doesn't he?"

"Well, I don't think he's putting any weight on it, but he's drinking. God, look at him, he's going to burst!"

"We'd better make sure he doesn't overdo it. Careful, boy, not so fast."

"Oh, he'll be okay," said Audrey, then, the smile slowly fading from her face, her hands searching for the pockets of her dressing gown, she looked up from the neck-extended, tongue-flickering drinker and held Jane's face with her eyes.

"What?" said Jane.

But she knew.

As she asked the question, she knew.

"I still don't understand," said Audrey. "I still don't understand what happened, Plain. You said . . . You said you *hit* him, in a car. I mean, what . . . ? What car were you *talking* about? Plain, what car did you *mean*?"

30

Slk, slk, slk, slk went Aziz's rough tongue against the milk. In its recess beyond the crockery cupboard, the heavy commercial refrigerator hummed. Light, from two fluorescent tubes, hung quivering over white tiles, scrubbed wood, Formica, over tea towels folded in damp, discolored piles, over cooking ranges and wooden plate racks and one gaudy

Spanish paperback novel, from whose pages a comb protruded, left there as a bookmark.

Jane was conscious of these peaceful things surrounding her, was conscious, also, of the smells: of soap suds, of potato peelings, of lingering, acrid sweat that dozed in the nighttime kitchen, but her central attention was focused on one object only, on the question that sat, awaiting its answer, in the firm, immovable grip of Audrey's eyes.

"What car were you *talking* about? Plain, what car did you *mean*?"

Why, why, why hadn't she realized, had she allowed herself to forget that this must come? From the moment when she'd broken down on the drive, from the moment when she'd said, "Oh, God, Augy," and shared the weight of her pain, the question had been inevitable and she must, now, answer it.

But how?

For God's sake, *how*?

If she lied to protect her friend, if she said, "What? Oh, some man's car. Just some man. I don't know. I was coming back from ringing my parents and he offered to give me a lift. . . ." If she said *that*, then she would at once destroy the seedlings of trust and love that the night had begun to sow. Even if Audrey believed her, *she* would know that she'd lied, would despise herself for having done so, hate Audrey for having made her.

Yet, were she to tell the truth, what then? What would remain of their awakening trust in each other then?

No, far better to lie. To protect Audrey, to protect her from . . . What? And *why*? Why did Audrey need protecting more than *she* did? They were equal, weren't they? Hadn't

235

the night proved that? And hadn't they, therefore, an equal right to the truth?

If Audrey decided to hate Jane for what she'd done, for what she'd made Gary do, well, that must be *her* decision. Mustn't it? Jane couldn't *control* her, manipulate her feelings. She hadn't the right to. Just as Audrey would have no right to do so to her. *That* wasn't friendship, surely.

Jane's lungs were still stretching for air. Her lips were still parting. Two yards away from her, on the far side of the kitchen table, on the far side of the piedish and the straining, slurping kitten, Audrey's gaze was still quick with the question which, one second ago, it couldn't be more than one second ago, she had asked.

"What car did you . . . ?"

"Look, Aug," said Jane, "it was Gary's car."

She'd said it. Right or wrong, she'd said it. And if, seeing seep into Audrey's face a confusion of shock, anger, hurt, incredulity, Jane wished that she'd spoken differently, she also knew that she couldn't, mustn't, go back. Neither apologies, nor gratuitous explanations, nor a barrage of justifications must now be allowed to intervene between Audrey and the truth.

She clenched her hands and bit together her lips.

"Gary's?" asked Audrey. "*My* Gary's? *Henny*'s Gary? I mean . . . Gary?"

"Yes," said Jane.

"But . . . What on earth are you talking about? How can it've been? What do you mean? You were *driving Gary's car*?"

"Yes."

"But when?"

236

"The day . . ."

"On Tuesday? Is that what you mean? Is that what you were doing when you skipped off games? Is that what you mean? You were driving with Gary?"

"Yes," said Jane. "I rang him and asked him to come. . . ."

"For a *drive*?"

"No!"

"Well *what* then? Don't smile like that. *What* then? How am I supposed to know. I mean, why on earth *should* he . . . ?"

"I asked him to. I asked him to, Augy. I was . . ."

"What?"

There fell a silence; in the course of which, Aziz withdrew from the piedish, slumped back onto his haunches, raised his head and stretched his jaws in a yawn. The refrigerator continued to rattle and hum.

"I was unhappy," said Jane, at last. "I was lonely and . . . I was unhappy. Look, I didn't know who else . . . I mean, there *wasn't* anyone else. I know I'd made it that way. I know I'd deliberately shut myself up. But . . ."

"No you hadn't," said Audrey.

"Yes I had. I mean, you know, that row in the basement. I did sort of *make* it happen. You must know that. I sort of *wanted* it to happen, really, I suppose. I . . ."

"Yes, okay, but that wasn't what started it, was it?" said Audrey.

"What d'you mean?"

"It was the weekend, wasn't it? You know, when I . . ."

Suddenly, Audrey clenched her face, swung away from

237

Jane and gripped the rim of the sinks. She leaned her waist against the sinks and let her head drop forward.

"Aug?"

"Look, just tell me what happened. You rang Gary and then what? He said he'd come down."

"I didn't just *ask* him, Aug. I was crying. I was hysterical. . . ."

So, piece by piece, answer by answer, Jane reconstructed for Audrey the events of the previous Tuesday.

On the black windowpanes above the sinks, disks of rain had begun to appear with a tiptoe, pattering sound.

"So," said Audrey at last, her back still turned towards Jane, her voice muffled and thick, "you waited till lights out, then set off to look for him."

"Yes," said Jane.

"Did you think you'd find him?"

"No, not . . . His body? Yes. Yes, I *had* to."

Audrey grunted. A dead coal fell through a grate. Against the glass of the kitchen windows, the raindrops accelerated, grew louder.

Jane waited.

Audrey sighed. She unclenched her fingers from the sinks' china rim and tipped her weight onto her heels. She straightened up. She turned around.

For a second, then, Jane thought that the verdict was about to be given, that judgment was about to be pronounced. But Audrey's eyes, as they skimmed Jane's face, as they drifted away from Jane's face to the sleeping kitten on the table, were drawn, opaque curtains.

"Aziz," she said, and her voice was as dull as her eyes. "Aziz."

The kitten awoke, yawned, stretched, dragged his injured leg beneath his body and staggered, disorientated but willing, to his feet. Audrey lifted him from the table.

"I'm taking him outside," she said. "He'd better, after all that milk he's drunk."

Jane could have answered, "But he was asleep. He was all right."

Instead, she nodded twice and said nothing. She let them both go, Audrey and the kitten, because they weren't hers to restrain. Their lives, their thoughts, their opinions were independent of her and of her will.

She'd shared the truth. Now, she *mustn't* attempt to monopolize, or to control, the reaction to that truth.

She heard the kitchen door click shut behind her. She saw the raindrops crowd on the windows' black glass and heard the wind groan. Tiredness like a blanket enfolded her brain. Her face was burning. Her eyelids were swollen and aching.

She walked to the kitchen table. She lifted herself onto the table and, having pushed to one side the piedish, lay down and slept.

31

It'd stopped raining and the light behind the windows was gray when Audrey woke her.

"*What?*" she said, floundering, grabbing at air.

"Shh," said Audrey. "Don't shout. I think the maids are arriving."

"What?"

She knew where she was. She was on a kitchen table. Head aching, throat sore, she was lying on a table in the middle of the school kitchen, beneath two fluorescent light tubes. But *why* was she there? Hadn't it . . . ? Wasn't it something to do . . . ?

"Where's Aziz?" she asked, sitting up, knocking a china piedish with the wrist of her left hand.

"He's all right," said Audrey. "He's just eating some sardines. Look."

"Oh, yes."

"Come on, then. Get up. The maids're going to be here in a second. I think their bus has just arrived."

"Yes, right," said Jane, feeling around her as though for a hat, or a pair of gloves, then staring once more at Audrey. There was something that she had to remember.

"Come *on*."

"Okay," she said. "But . . . What are we going to do? I mean . . ."

There was something that they had to do.

"We're going to take Aziz to the Termite, aren't we?" said Audrey. "Come on. Hurry up. We'll wait outside her drawing room. I'd rather do that than go and find her in her bedroom, don't you think?"

"Yes, I suppose so."

Jane frowned. A pneumatic hammer was beating inside her head. Her face burned and her eyes ached from the light. She shivered, then sneezed, the explosion tearing her throat with iron claws.

"Oh, God, don't say you've gone and got a cold."

"No, I'm all right," she said. "But look, listen Augy, you

240

can't come with me. I mean, why *should* you?"

"Because I want to. Okay?"

"But don't be stupid. What are we going to say? We can't say we were *both* driving the car, can we? Anyway, you weren't. You weren't there. I'm not letting you take the blame for something you . . . ."

"What the *hell*'re you talking about, girl? You're not seriously suggesting . . . Don't be mad! Plain, the Termite mustn't find out what *actually* happened. We're only telling her *anything* because, otherwise, there'd be all sorts of questions and inquiries and other people getting into trouble. If it weren't for that, we could just leave Aziz in her room for her to find. But if she knew what had *actually* . . . No, listen, for goodness' sake, we'll just say we found him, tonight. We slipped out to make a phone call and we found him, in the woods. I mean, it's almost true, damn it, and we'll certainly get into quite enough trouble. . . ."

"No," said Jane. "I've got to tell her the truth."

She slid from the table. She walked to where Aziz was crouching with his nose in a tin of sardines. She scooped the kitten up into her arms.

"I've got to do it, Aug. After all, I told *you* the truth and . . ."

"But that's different."

"Why is it?"

"Because . . . Well, if you don't *see* why it is . . . But you do realize, don't you, what'll happen to Gary, if you tell the Termite he came down here to see you and let you drive his car?"

"I can't help it."

"What do you damn well mean, you can't help it? Of course you bloody well can."

"I can't," said Jane, aware that she was beginning to cry; not convulsively, but as though her eyes no longer had the strength to hold her tears in place.

"*Why* can't you . . . ?"

"Shh. The maids. They're here."

"Damn! Come on, let's get out of this place. Have you got . . . ? Right."

Audrey opened the kitchen door. At the far end of the passageway, in the glass-domed entrance hall, a group of a half-dozen women was laughing, talking, unbuttoning coats and unknotting bright, patterned head scarves.

"Quick," said Audrey. "Before they come. Down into the basement."

"But they'll see the sardines. And the piedish."

"It doesn't matter. It'll be hours before they get around to telling anyone and, by that time . . . Quick, come on."

Breath held, mouths stretched ajar, eyes fixed like hooks to the jovial, treacherous group five yards away from them, they left the kitchen and slipped down the basement stairs. Two seconds later, like a gate closing over their heads, came the slapping of feet and the swelling of deep, careless voices.

The kitchen door clicked open.

The voices paused, then exploded on a new, shriller note.

The kitchen door closed. The voices were absorbed in its thickness.

"Right," said Audrey, wriggling against the tightness of the cubbyhole halfway down the basement stairs into which she, Jane and the kitten had jammed themselves. "Let's just give them a minute or two to get frying, or whatever. As

242

soon as they've started work, they won't be able to hear anything for the clatter.

"Aziz all right?" she asked, rotating the cramp from her shoulders, swiveling her back in an effort to make it more comfortable.

"Yes," said Jane. "Augy?"

"Okay. I heard. You're going to tell the Termite the truth, the whole truth and nothing but the truth. Well done. I heard you the first time."

"But don't you see why, Aug? I mean, what else can I do? Maybe you wish I hadn't told *you*, either, but. . . ."

"Listen, I'd rather assumed that the reason you'd told *me* was because we were friends. That was what I'd thought. Okay? I was wrong. So let's just drop the subject."

"No! You *weren't* wrong. That *was* why I told you. That was *just* . . ."

"So you're telling the Termite for the same reason. Is that it? Your good old friend the Termite."

"Of course not. It's just that . . . I mean, all right, I don't even *like* her. As a matter of fact, I hate her guts. But . . . I mean, she's still got a right to the *truth*, hasn't she?"

"You tell me."

"I don't *know*. That's why I'm asking you, damn it."

"Who does know? Who does, for God's sake? If you ask me, you can only ever tell what was right or what was wrong afterwards, by the results. I mean, in this case, okay, you're not *supposed* to tell lies. But you're not supposed to hurt people, either, are you? Or get people into trouble. So, how do you decide which is the most important?"

"That's just it," said Jane. "I don't know. I suppose . . .

I suppose it *varies*, depending on the circumstances. I mean, I suppose you have to decide that again, every time. Going by what seems the most important to you, or something."

"Sounds reasonable enough to me," said Audrey, and Jane saw her smiling.

"But . . . but God," she said. "Why *isn't* there just one set of rules? I mean, it's so . . . it's so bloody *hard*. And it means you can never tell, really, whether you *have* got it right. Not until afterwards, like you said . . ."

"Well, there are some things you know jolly *well* are wrong."

"Yes, of course, but between one right and another . . . ? Oh, hell, Aug, I'm so tired. My . . . my head . . . my . . . I can't *think* anymore."

As well as she could within the confines of the cubbyhole, Audrey twisted towards Jane.

"Here," she said. "Here, let me feel. Hey! Have you felt your face?"

"No."

"It's like an oven. I think you've got a temperature, Plain. Don't you feel hot? You must. You're burning."

"Am I? I don't know."

"I'm telling you."

"Aug, look, listen, maybe you're right. About telling the Termite. You are. You're right. We'll just . . . We'll just say . . . What? That we were in Eliston's Woods? That we'd gone out to make a telephone call and . . . ?"

"Yes," said Audrey, softly. "Yes. We heard him meowing or something. Something like that. You know."

She withdrew her hand from Jane's face, but not her eyes. These darted across the other's features with the same intense curiosity as that with which they had several times already that night, as though they kept on seeing her for the first time.

"But why have you changed your mind?" she asked.

Jane closed her eyes, then opened them. She looked at Audrey, returning Audrey's frown, reflecting the puzzled bow of Audrey's eyebrows, the clench of muscles around her searching eyes.

"Because, in this instance, I prefer to lie to the Termite than to hurt you," she said. "I don't know if that's right, but she's getting Aziz back and . . . and *he*'s okay. . . . I mean, *he* doesn't give a damn what I say or what I don't. . . . So . . . Well . . . That's why."

"Thanks," said Audrey. "I just wouldn't've wanted Henny to . . ."

"Yes, I know. And, for God's sake, don't thank me."

"Why not? It's about time I started being a bit nice to you, don't you think?"

"You always have been."

"Rubbish."

"Well, that was only because I *let* you bully me. Made you, in a way. A sort of game, wasn't it? A sort of . . . parts we were playing. Not the real us. I think it's only tonight that I've started realizing there *is* a real you. And look what you've done for me. . . . No, I'm serious, you jolly well *didn't* have to come and find Aziz with me. And . . . For goodness' sake, Augy, you do realize that if you come with me to the Termite we're both going to get into the most awful trouble?"

"A lot less than if you went alone," said Audrey, laughing. "Your ideas on how to handle that woman! Honestly. And in

245

the state you're in now, you could drive her to murder, I shouldn't wonder. Anyway, the worst she can do is expel us and then, think, finishing school in Switzerland! Men! Freedom! That sort of trouble I can cope with. Can't you?"

"Don't joke about it."

"I'm not joking. Besides, can't you just imagine what sort of fun I'd have, if you were kicked out and I had to stay? Nicky probably won't ever be talking to me again and as for the others! I mean, however infuriating you are, Plain, at least you're not boring."

"I am," said Jane. "Quite often. I even bore myself, sometimes."

"Well, you know best. But you're boring in an interesting way, and that's something. The complications you manage to create, out of just getting through life! Extraordinary!"

Through the pounding of her head, through the shivering of her body, Jane smiled. Her smile spread to Audrey.

"Aren't I right?" asked Audrey.

"Yes," said Jane, shifting the kitten in her arms, taking one more look at Audrey, absorbing the strength from her face.

"Well then," she said, at last, "I suppose we'd better be going. Put our poor heads on the block. Are you ready to do your charming-the-old-lady act? You're never going to need it more, I can tell you."

"Don't worry. One look at my beautiful, tortured, young face and the Termite'll melt onto the carpet."

"You'd better be right."

"Go on. Get down."

Jane said, "Do you want to carry Aziz?"

"Well . . . No. You do, don't you?"

"No," said Jane. "You hold him. After all, it's . . . Come on, you take him."

The kitten was passed from one pair of arms to the other, as, clumsily, stiff from their incarceration, the two girls lowered themselves from the cubbyhole to the stairs. Above them, the clinking of plates and cutlery sounded muffled behind a closed door. Then a bell rang.

"Quick," said Jane.

"Okay. I'm ready. Come on."

As they reached the entrance hall, Miss Anthony, her hair freshly combed from her face, her brown shoes gleaming like chestnuts, her neat hands ensnaring a pile of dog-eared exercise books, was descending the marble staff staircase.

"Miss Anthony?"

32

Sleep; surfacing now and again towards consciousness, towards sharp, stabbing lights, the rack of movements and noise, the pain of cloth against oversensitive skin; then sleep again.

Voices:

"How're you feeling, Jane? Comfortable? That's right. Now, open your mouth. Under the tongue. Don't bite. . . ."

"Dear me, still rather high, I'm afraid. . . ."

"A touch of fever, the doctor says, aggravated by undernourishment. She'll be all right with a few days' rest.

He's prescribed some antibiotics. . . ."

"Come on, now, Jane, sit up. Just a little bit of scrambled egg. There's a good girl. Just a bit more. One for mummy, one for daddy, one for matron . . ."

Then dark, disintegrating sleep again.

Waking to sweat, to pajamas soaked with sweat. The pillow's sodden when she lifts her face and there's water in the cups behind her collar bones, in the crease of her elbows, in the hollow at the back of her knees. Between her pointed shoulder blades, there's a patch of wetness the size of an exercise book.

And she's weak. Walking to the loo, her legs collapse beneath her. She has to lean against a wall, has to shuffle along with the aid of the wall, takes hours unknotting her dressing-gown cord, pulling her pajama bottoms down. When she gets back to her bed, they've changed the sheets. The new ones are crisp and cold. She crashes against them, electric pain running through her limbs to her neck, chin and eyes.

Then, once again, sleep takes over. Generous and deep, it receives her without question. She has only to imagine it for it to be there; in the beginning, anyway.

Because, after a while, the periods of unconsciousness began to get, if not shorter, or less frequent, shallower. Jane found that she was no longer able to submerge herself in them. Her eyes would close, her body would begin to relax, but what had previously been nothingness had become, now, a soft, constant whispering, a flickering of pictures, a building up, layer upon layer, of memory, thought and emotion.

For a start, the bed, and the room in which the bed was, insisted on acquiring an identity. Jane was forced to accept that she existed in a space that was specific, that was at a fixed and measurable distance from other specific places. She wasn't merely in bed, she was in a bed in the isolation room of the school infirmary. Ten yards along the corridor was where the more jovial under-matron slept and, beyond that, past a green baize door, down a short flight of stairs, was the corridor in which her own dormitory was situated, in which Audrey's dormitory was situated and where, it now being night, Audrey would be curled up asleep.

Or would she be? What had happened to her since that moment, when, as they were leaving the Termite's drawing room, the jovial under-matron had come hurrying towards them, had aborted their privacy, had called, "Jane! There you are. You're a very naughty girl, now aren't you? Didn't I tell you to come and see me before breakfast? And what are you doing downstairs in your pajamas? You, too, Audrey. What's this all about? Upstairs! Upstairs with the two of you! Come along, Jane, I'm going to put you on the scales this very instant."

Oh, it had been all right for Jane. With the under-matron's encouragement, Jane had escaped, into shivering, burning, crying, a temperature of a hundred and four degrees and bed.

But what had happened to Audrey? Had she gone on to breakfast? Exhausted as she, too, must've been, had she taken the French exam? And with whom had she been able to share that scene in the headmistress's drawing room? The memory of the Termite's burning, red eyelids, of her face's contractions as she fought and fought against tears, the memory of her voice, of the loathing in her voice, when she'd said, "Just go. Both of you, just leave me. Get *out*. If you think I'm going to thank you . . . Just go! I don't know what . . . I don't know what this is all about, where you've been all night, what *really* . . . But just get out, will you? Get out of here. Go on. Get out, out, out!"

How had Audrey been able to carry, unshared, the shock of that hatred, or the shock of that lust when the Termite had snatched Aziz from her arms and, deaf to his squeals, had clamped him against her neat, tweed bust, had plunged beneath his fur her clawing, pale, oval fingernails?

Why, for heaven's sake, hadn't Audrey come to see Jane, to talk to her? Had it been forbidden? Had she not *wanted* to come?

As, hour after hour, the ropes of her awakening consciousness tightened around Jane's brain, she twisted and turned through the night. When breakfast came, on its stained, plastic tray, she made herself eat all of it in an attempt to exhaust her restlessness. She even asked for a second slice of bread.

"Well, you are feeling better today, aren't you? Your temperature's down a bit, too. Almost normal. Maybe you'll be able to get up a bit this morning. Have a little walk around. Not far. Just up and down the corridor."

"Yes," said Jane. "All right. And, I wonder, do you think someone could come to see me?"

"*See* you, poppet? What about?"

"No, I just meant . . . You know. A friend. It's awfully boring with no one to talk to. Honestly."

"We'll see," said the jollier under-matron, spreading Jane's bread with marmalade, then cutting the soggy slice into four equal parts. "There, let me see you put that down you."

Then she said, "I'll have to ask Miss Anthony, you know. Of course, she's as pleased as Punch that the kitten's been found, but I don't think she's quite so happy about *how* you and Audrey Croft came to find him. That was very, very silly. You know that, don't you?"

Jane lowered to its plate the marmalade-heavy triangle that she'd been about to bite. Slowly, unaware of what she was doing, she licked her fingers and thumb.

She looked up at the under-matron, at her pert, raised, right eyebrow, at her pursed lips and the dimple by the corner of her mouth. She couldn't believe that the woman had said what she'd heard.

". . . she's as pleased as Punch that the kitten's been found . . . don't think she's quite so happy about *how* you and Audrey Croft came to find him. . . ."

Pleased as Punch? Not quite so happy? What had those expressions to do with the awfulness of all that had happened?

"You do *know* you've been silly, don't you, Jane?" repeated the under-matron and Jane almost shouted, "Silly? Is *that* what you call it? Is that what *everyone*'s calling it?"

Instead, she said, "Yes. Yes, I suppose I have. I *know* I have. I'm sorry. I'm sorry if I've caused you a lot of trouble, too."

"Oh, that's all right. That's what I'm here for, after all."

"But do you think I could, though? Have a visitor? I mean, do you think Augy could just pop up and see me, quickly? In a break or something? Do you think you could ask her?"

251

33

For a moment, as Audrey closed the isolation room door behind her, as she straightened up, turned around and looked at Jane across the room, it was as though the two of them were strangers. The one wore a uniform, smelled of the school, had just come from tea, or games, or a lesson in the courtyard classroom. The other lay surrounded by signs of exclusivity: medicine, fruit, a book about ponies open across her lap. They seemed to have nothing in common, not even a language.

"Hi," said Audrey.

"Hello, Aug," said Jane.

She closed the book about ponies. She searched for somewhere to put it. She slid it, finally, beneath her tea tray.

"How're you feeling?" asked Audrey.

"Fine," said Jane. "Well . . . How are you?"

"*I*'m all right."

Footsteps clicked along the corridor. Jane held her breath. No one, no one must come in now. No one must come in now and see this: two school friends embarrassed at meeting beyond the school timetable, lost, with nothing to say. If this were seen, by the under-matron, by anyone, it might become true. It *would* become true.

The footsteps passed. At the end of the passageway, the green baize door squeaked open upon its hinges, then thudded once, twice, shut against its jamb.

Jane breathed. She raked the damp hair from her forehead.

"Augy," she said.

"Yup?"

"What's been . . . ? Has it . . . ? Augy, I'm *sorry* I opted out on you like this."

"I told you you were ill, didn't I?" said Audrey. Then she smiled. Then she removed her hands from the pockets of her skirt and walked forwards into the room.

Sending flying to the floor a box of paper handkerchiefs, Jane slid to one side of her bed.

"You can sit here if you want. I don't think I'm catching. Augy, what's it been like? Have you had to see the Termite again? What's she said? All *I* get is that she's . . ."

"Calm down! Look at you! For goodness' sake!"

"Okay, okay, but have you *seen* her again? The Termite? Have you? Oh, it was *awful*, wasn't it?"

"Yes," said Audrey. "Yes, it wasn't a lot of fun. Still . . ."

She shrugged.

She said, "She didn't believe us. You know that, don't you? She knew jolly well we there was something we weren't telling her. But what could she do? She couldn't prove anything and, besides, she didn't know *what*, exactly, it was she *should* be proving. And she'd got Aziz back. That's really all she cares about. So . . . So, anyway, the whole thing's going to be forgotten. No thanks. No questions. No punishment. Quits."

"Nothing? Nothing at *all*?"

"Nope."

"That's that?"

"Yup."

"But . . ."

"What? What, Plain?"

"It just doesn't . . ."

"What? What would you've preferred? A public flogging? Jeering mobs and flagellation? Why? What'd be the point? If it's punishment you're after, you've already *done* that, yourself."

"I just don't see why I should get *away* with it, that's all. It isn't right. It isn't fair."

"Look, Plain, it's over. It's done with. Can't we just . . . ?"

"Forget it?"

"No. Don't be stupid. But . . . Oh!"

Audrey threw up her arms and stamped with one foot on the floor. "I *knew* you'd react like this! Plain, why can't you just be *happy* for once? Aziz is *okay*. Isn't that all that matters? Why can't we just . . . ?"

"I'm sorry, Aug," said Jane.

She lay back and closed her eyes.

No, it *wasn't* all that mattered. There was something else, something that had been there before even she'd hit Aziz, before even she'd telephoned Gary, before even . . .

"Plain? You're not sleeping, are you?"

"No," she said. "Of course not."

"Look, here, I forgot to give you these."

Jane opened her eyes, to see Audrey sitting beside her, fishing for something in the right-hand pocket of her skirt.

"A couple of letters that came for you yesterday. I got them off Old Bailey."

"Oh, thanks," said Jane, turning the letters faceup, seeing that one was from her godmother in New Zealand and the other, the other, the other . . .

"What's the matter now? Hey, Plain Face, what is it? Are you all right? Look, come on. D'you want me to get the matron?"

Jane said, "It's from my father."

"So? What *about* it?"

"I . . . I don't know. I feel sick. I think I'm going to be sick."

"For heaven's sake! What . . . ? *Oh*," said Audrey. "Oh, I see. You think . . . About your mama. Plain, look, give it to me, I'll read it first."

"No."

"But you're going to *have* to open it."

"No."

"But . . . Look, if it was something serious, he'd have *rung* you. He wouldn't just've . . . Let me open it, Plain."

"No! It's not that! It's . . ."

Jane pushed the sheets and blankets from her body. She was drenched in a new sweat. Between the fingers and thumb of her right hand, she could feel the smooth solidity of the letter, but she couldn't look at it. She couldn't look again at the neat, rectangular, typewritten address, the stamp with the Kentish postmark.

As though it were a wind-filled tunnel, her brain was sucking her into itself, was sucking her backwards past pictures and smells and sounds; past the Termite's twisted face; past her voice screaming, "Out, out, out!" Past Aziz, lapping milk, limping through Eliston's Woods, hurtling, his mouth torn open, across the windscreen of Gary's car; past the burnt, aromatic smell of Gary's cheroots, the music

255

of his voice. "Cry it all out of you, then. That's right. Let it go. Nobody's going to hear you." Past Mrs. Croft and Henrietta, to a Tuesday afternoon, after lunch, when trollies rattled between dining room and kitchen, when maids laughed, when sunlight dropped through the glass dome of the school entrance hall and Mrs. Bailey called, ". . . Bacham? Beaching?"

"Rackham! It's me, Mrs. Bailey. Here!"

"Darling Janey, You'd have thought, after all the practice she's had, that your mama would've been able to produce her seventh child without any problems at all. . . . So, you see that you're well out of all this. . . ."

"I *hated* him, Augy. I hated them *all.* I wanted . . . I didn't . . . Augy, I didn't care if he . . . If the baby . . . If he *died*, Augy. Diggory. My brother. I didn't . . . I wanted them *all* to die. Him, Mummy, Daddy . . . Why should *they* be together? Why should they assume that *I*'d be all right? That *I* was okay, that . . . I mean, nobody asked her to go on having all those children. Why couldn't she have just stopped with . . . ? Why is it always *me* who has to look after myself, who has to look after the others, who has to cope? Why am *I* always supposed to be fine? *I* can go to boarding school. Becky's too nervous, but I'm all right. I *have* to damn well be. I'm the eldest. What . . . ? What else can I . . . ?"

Jane stopped. Her head was burning, was thundering with pain. Around her, the isolation room swam slowly back into focus. She saw the bed again, the runkled blankets, the upturned box of paper handkerchiefs on the floor, Audrey, Audrey's uniform, the ink stains on Audrey's index finger and middle finger and thumb.

"Oh, God," she said.

"It's no better being the younger of two," said Audrey, "I can tell you."

"I'm sorry, I didn't mean any of that."

"Of course you did."

"I didn't. I didn't know what I was saying."

"You still meant it. It doesn't matter, Plain. What d'you think? Everybody hates their parents sometimes."

"That's not true."

"Well, there are times when *I* hate my mother, anyway."

"Yes, but that's . . ."

"What?" said Audrey.

Jane touched her eyelids. The beat of pain in her head was slower now, was softer, was becoming easier to bear.

She said, "I meant, it's not really *hate*, that, what you feel."

"Yes it is. Sometimes. Except it's not actually her I hate, of course. It's more the possessiveness, the clinging, you know."

"Yes. Yes, I suppose . . . I don't know. Maybe *either* way . . ."

"What?"

"Parents. Maybe, whether they're clinging, or, you know, like mine . . . Maybe it's not *them* at all, but *us*. Whether they hold on too long or let go too soon . . . I mean, the separation, the realizing that you're a separate *person*, that you're on your own . . . Maybe it's *always* difficult. Oh, God, Augy, I feel terrible."

"Don't. There's no need."

"There is. Look, Gary said that to me, about growing up, about admitting that you're a person, a strong, competent person, able to make decisions, you know, and take responsibility. But I wouldn't . . . I didn't want to *believe* it. It was . . . I don't know . . . Easier to blame my parents, I suppose. Oh, and you and him, too. Everyone. Anyone. For not looking after me properly. Instead of seeing that it was up to me now . . ."

"Gary seems to have said quite a lot of things to you," said Audrey.

"What?" said Jane. "Oh, I'm sorry, Aug. I didn't think."

"Don't be stupid. It doesn't matter. I was joking, Plain."

Audrey tugged at Jane's pajama collar.

"I was joking, honestly. It just takes a bit of getting used to, the idea of you and Henny's husband having deep, passionate talks in Eliston's Woods. That's all."

"But Augy, you know it was only because I sort of blackmailed him. He'd never have come if I hadn't . . ."

"Yes, I know all that. You told me. And I promise I don't mind. Only, you're not . . . ? You know. You don't love him, or . . ."

"No. Not like that. I did *think* I did, mind you. But I was just doing the same to him as I was to you and to my parents. Asking him to protect me, look after me, you know. In fact, if you think about it, you've only yourself to blame. If you hadn't been so beastly to me that weekend . . ."

"Rubbish!"

"Yes," said Jane, laughing. "Rubbish."

"I should jolly well think so. Now, go on, open your papa's letter."

Slowly, Jane raised her right hand from where it lay, beside her, on the mattress. She looked at the square, white envelope, at the rectangle of type. Then she stood the letter on the bedside table, propped between her teacup and the medicine bottle, and said, "No. No, not yet."

She untucked her feet from the runkle of blankets that imprisoned them.

"Hey, hand me that dressing gown, Aug."

"Why? Where are you going?"

"Isn't there a telephone along there, in the matron's room?"

"I don't know. Yes, I think so. Yes, there is."

"I'm going to ring my mother."

"You're what? What do you mean? You're just going to . . . D'you mean you're just going to ring her, like that, without asking anyone?"

"That's exactly what I mean."

"But you don't even . . . I mean, she may not be home yet. She may still be in the hospital."

"Well, if she is, I'll get the number off Daddy. I just . . . I'm going to talk to her. Ask her how she is. Tell her *I'm* all right. Nothing . . . Nothing important. And nothing to do with *this* letter, either. To do with the last one. I never answered it. Did you know?"

"No," said Audrey. "No, I didn't. Well then, off you go! It's about bloody time you did."

"Yes. Yes, you're right. Hey, chuck me that dressing gown, will you? Please?"

259

34

It was the last day of term. The trunks had been packed. Since early morning, the good-byes had been shouted from dormitory to dormitory, the letters had been promised, the lost treasures rediscovered at the back of drawers, cupboards, desks.

At lunch, a first-former had vomited with excitement.

After lunch, the awards for tidiness, good conduct and academic success had been pronounced, by a cool, neat, benevolent, smiling headmistress.

Now, at half past four in the afternoon, the school was contained inside the entrance hall, awaiting the bus and the cavalcade of liberating parental cars.

"Silence! Silence, girls," called Miss MacKenzie.

Mrs. Bailey called, "Quiet! Be quiet! Or you'll none of you be going home at all."

Jane Rackham stood propped against the newel post at the bottom of the marble staff staircase. Audrey Croft sat on the second step, beside her.

"So," said the latter, "another jolly hollies, what? Another end, another beginning. Brings a lump to your throat, doesn't it?"

"It most certainly does," said Jane Rackham.

"Makes you think about all those who've been before and all those who'll come after. That glorious regiment of blue-skirted girlhood . . ."

"Enjoying, unbeknownst to them, the happiest days of

their lives. Days on which they'll look back . . ."

"Don't *say* that," said Audrey, her voice abruptly dropping from its previous, lilting disguise. "Not even in jest, do you hear me?"

"Yes, okay, I hear you," said Jane. "What's the matter?"

"Well, can you imagine, if these *are* the happiest days, I mean, what's the *rest* going to be like?"

"Good question."

"No, it's not. It's . . . Look, Plain, after next term, after O levels, are you going to be staying on here?"

"What's that got to do with anything?"

"Nothing. Just something I was thinking about."

"Well, no, I don't suppose I will. I don't think I want to, anyway. Another two years? No. If I go on to take A levels, which I suppose I will, I won't really want to. . . . Not *here*. *You* know."

"*I*'ve wanted to get out for ages."

"It's not so much a question of wanting to get out. More . . . I don't know, it's almost as though I've been *squeezed* out, in a way. Do you know what I mean? This term, Aziz and . . . Well, everything. It's like suddenly finding you've got too big for a pair of shoes or something."

"I know what you mean."

"But it hasn't been *all* awful, Aug. Has it? I'm jolly happy now, for example."

"Oh, I suppose not. Marginally better than a concentration camp, I daresay. Or prison. Look, what I'm saying is, are we going to bump into each other, when we've left?"

"Yes," said Jane. "Of course. Why not?"

"I just wondered."

Jane frowned. She pushed her weight from the newel post

261

on which she'd been leaning and moved around to sit beside Audrey on the marble step.

"I don't suppose you'd like to come and stay at my place, for a few days during the holidays, would you?" she asked.

"What? This holidays?"

"Yes."

"But what about your mama? With the baby and everything?"

"Well, I'll ask her, but I'm sure she won't mind. She's really much better. And so's he, old Diggory. Daddy says you'd never guess he'd been on death's doorstep, the noise he makes. I can't wait to see him. When I rang . . . *You* know . . . He was even screaming then. I could hear him in the background. God, Aug, I'm so *glad.* . . . Oh, you know what I mean."

"Yes," said Audrey. She smiled. "All letters answered, eh, old Plain Face? No more terrible guilt and moaning."

"*No* more? No, I shouldn't say that. Give me till tomorrow. I'll find *something* else to feel bad about."

"God, no, not that soon, please."

"Well . . ."

They laughed with one another. Beyond them, in the entrance hall, the door was being pushed open as the first cars crunched across the gravel.

"It's Mummy!" shouted a bucktoothed, red-headed first-former. "Mrs. Bailey, good-bye! Good-bye, Miss MacKenzie! Suzy! Clarky! I'll see you next term. Mummy, I'm here."

Then Ruth Bottomly emerged from the crowd, to punch Jane's shoulder.

" 'Bye, Plain. 'Bye, Augy. See you next term. My

folks have just arrived. Have a good hols."

" 'Bye, Bummly."

" 'Bye, Bummly."

Mrs. Bailey shouted, "Order please!"

"Augy! Plain! 'Bye!" called Miranda Spurling, her round face bobbing on the sea of blue sweaters and coats.

" 'Bye, Randy!"

Mrs. Bailey shouted, "The school bus is here! Will all those traveling by train please assemble around the table?"

"That's you," said Jane.

Audrey stood.

"Yes, I know," she said. "Well . . ."

"I'll ring you tomorrow, about you coming to stay."

"Will you?"

"Of course. But, what about *your* mama, Augy?"

"What about her? She won't kill you. Not over the telephone, anyway."

"No, don't be stupid. I meant, will she mind? If you come and stay with me? They're not *awfully* long holidays, are they? You know, from her point of view."

"I'll talk to her. It'll be okay. I'm . . . Oh, you know, you've got to understand her. What with my father . . . Well . . . Hey, do you want me to send your love to Gary?"

"Don't be vile."

"For the last *time*! Will all those girls traveling by train please assemble around the table? I want to check your names. The bus is waiting."

"Well, 'bye then," said Jane. "Look after yourself and all that rubbish. And don't overeat tonight."

Audrey smiled, touched Jane's hand, laughed and began to turn. Then, as though her eyes had been snatched by a

263

magnet, she swung around towards Jane again. But it was over Jane's shoulder that she was looking, beyond her, up the staircase.

"Do you see what I've seen?" she whispered.

Jane, too, swiveled around and there, eleven steps up, at the landing where the marble staff staircase turned a right angle, eyes enormous, tail swishing, ears twitching to the babble from the entrance hall, sat Aziz.

"Look at him. As fat as a damn plum pudding. You'd think he'd never . . ."

"I bet he's forgotten all about it."

"I bet he has, too."

"I even think his leg's better."

"It is. I saw him trying to catch a squirrel on the lawn this morning. Moved as though he'd never limped in his life."

"I suppose he *hasn't* ever, really," said Jane. "I mean, if he can't remember it."

"Audrey Croft! How many times have I got to call you, girl? The bus is waiting. We're going to miss the train."

When Audrey had gone, when she'd become just another blue shape, just another uniform, just another name to be ticked before the school bus could leave, Jane stood up from where she'd been sitting, turned around and knelt on the step. Aziz was still there.

Rubbing together the index finger and thumb of her right hand, "Aziz," she whispered.

The kitten stared at her.

"Aziz. Here, boy. Aziz."

The kitten rolled onto his back. He hollowed his back,

then sprang to his feet and skedaddled away, around the bend in the marble staff staircase. He ran unencumbered by past, unafraid of future. Guiltless, brave, irresponsible, he flicked the tip of his thick, black tail behind him.

He didn't have *nine* lives, that cat. He'd one for every second he breathed. Each moment, for him, was a new state of being, detached, independent, free.

Or was it free?

Pushing herself up from her knees, buttoning her coat, feeling in the pockets of her coat for the regulation leather gloves, Jane wasn't so sure.

After all, what sort of decisions could Aziz make, what sort of choices had he? What direction could he take with his "freedom"?

None. He stood at the mercy of every moment, at the whim of each scampering squirrel. Hunger, tiredness, the desire to have his ears scratched, all these could surprise and imprison him.

All right, so she, too, was a captive. She, too, had physical needs and emotional wants. But *she* was *aware* of this. *That* was the difference. And, being aware, she had also the power to control.

Her life was in *her* hands, to live, in fear, or courage, as *she* chose. And, unlike the kitten, she'd only one, one life. She must value every part of it, the shames as well as the pride, the fear as well as the happy anticipation. She must look at it, taste it, smell it, touch it, listen to its every rhythm. None of it must be avoided, not the mistakes, nor the pain, nor the humiliations. Nor the pleasures, either, the fact that her father would be arriving at any moment, that she'd be seeing her mother this evening, her brothers and

265

sisters and Diggory, that, soon, Audrey would be coming to stay with her. She mustn't let these be destroyed by lingerings of a stale, useless guilt. Experience must be a lesson, not a rope, not a chain.

And she *had* learned. Not everything, nothing like everything, but something. Talking on the telephone with her mother that day in the infirmary, hearing the joy in her own voice, the happiness free from resentment, talking to Audrey, feeling their friendship strengthen, grow, move forwards, Jane *knew* that she had learned.

Her coat was buttoned. Her gloves were on. She began to walk from the stairs to the body of the entrance hall. Reaching the entrance hall, she pressed her fingertips against a wall and raised herself to her toes. She peered above the chaos of moving, shouting heads.

No, all right, she wasn't free, not yet, but inside her lay the power to become so. Inside her lay the power to overcome fear. Inside her lay the power to love.

Past the open front door of the school slid a Land-Rover with a patched, canvas roof. Jane lowered herself to her heels.

"Excuse me. Hey, can I get through? Thanks. Miss MacKenzie, my father's arrived. Can I go now? My father's here," she said.

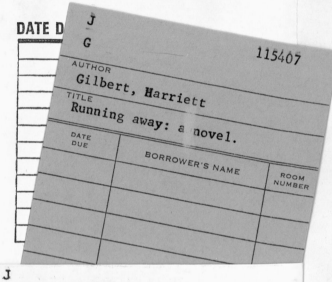